ACCLAIM FOR Alan Judd's

The Devil's Own Work

"Eloquent and daring. . . . A fine, intelligent work, an impious meditation on creativity and reality. One gets the sense that it must have been a wicked and joyful endeavor . . . it delights in mischief." —*Boston Globe*

"Literature, muses and the nature of creativity are the subjects of this novel. Enjoyable. . . . Filled with intelligence." —*Los Angeles Times*

"A brief return to the world of Faust, Mephistopheles and the Devil pact. Mr. Judd . . . achieves a deep polish." —Robert Grudin, *The New York Times Book Review*

"Elegantly succinct. . . . The secret of Mr. Judd's success is instantly apparent; this tightly written story eloquently suggests more than it explains." —*Wall Street Journal*

"Judd vividly and skillfully portrays the price to be paid by a writer who, too earnestly craving fame and fortune, is too willing to compromise himself to get it." —*Los Angeles Daily News*

Alan Judd

The Devil's Own Work

Alan Judd is the author of four previous novels as well as the critically acclaimed biography *Ford Madox Ford*. Educated at Oxford, he lives in London and works in the British Foreign Office.

INTERNATIONAL

The Devil's Own Work

The Devil's Own Work

A NOVEL BY

Alan Judd

Vintage International

VINTAGE BOOKS

A DIVISION OF RANDOM HOUSE, INC. NEW YORK

FIRST VINTAGE INTERNATIONAL EDITION,
JULY 1995

The Library of Congress has cataloged the Knopf edition
as follows:
Judd, Alan.
The devil's own work / Alan Judd.—1st American ed.
p. cm.
ISBN 0-679-42552-7
1. Spirit possession—France, Southern—Fiction.
2. Creation (Literary, artistic, etc.)—Fiction.
3. Authors—Fiction.
I. Title.
PR6060.U32D48 1994
823'.914—dc20   93-35934
CIP
Vintage ISBN: 0-679-74745-1

Author photograph © Tara Heinemann

Manufactured in the United States of America
10   9   8   7   6   5   4   3   2   1

to John and Janet
with my thanks

The Devil's Own Work

Chapter 1

❧ I HAD IT, you see, from Edward himself; though not all at once and never, I am sure, all of it. I don't suppose anyone could tell it all, except perhaps Eudoxie, and she was—is—part of the problem. The origins pre-date my marriage and Edward's fame. I now regard that time as our first youth but it seemed to us then, fresh from university and in London, the time of entry into full estate. Nothing was impossible and nothing unimagined, except failure. In my case you could say that I was merely wrong but Edward's is more complicated. He had every success an ambitious man could wish; it was the cost that got him.

Of course, when he purchased that particular ticket he had no idea—which of us could have?—of what compound interest can mean, over a lifetime. I don't suppose it even felt like a transaction, more another gift from a kindly Providence to add to his health, his looks, his charm, his winning disposition, his talent—

his genius, it came to be called, but I at least am more cautious now. Everyone liked, even loved him, or perhaps I should say that no one disliked him and everyone felt drawn to him. I think I loved him, though what it was in him that I loved I am only now beginning to grapple with. I also envied and for a while hated him but my knowledge of the price he paid makes it impossible for those feelings to last. And there is a coldness that slows my blood at the thought that he might still be paying it.

He had a flat in a Victorian house in Kennington, down one of those dirty Lambeth streets that for decades were described as "coming up" but which never quite seemed to arrive. I shared a flat with two other teachers in a modern block not far away. Edward was not a teacher, of course; from the start, he was to be a great writer. He never actually said as much but the knowledge of it somehow spread around him like a personal aura so that no one ever thought of him as anything else. Perhaps we assumed that you became a great writer simply by being intent on it and by keeping at it until your greatness became apparent. Perhaps even Edward assumed it. After all, the intellectual world is credulous enough to take many of us at our own evaluations and people can become very successful just by believing in themselves and so persuading everyone else. I think Edward did believe in himself.

4

He was lucky in that he had money from his father, so that while working on his first novel he didn't have to get a regular job but could do freelance reviewing, which was as useful for getting his name known as for what it earned. In those days there was nothing to distinguish him from the shoals of Eng. Lit. graduates who feed off the scraps of London publishing and journalism. The more fortunate and determined grow into big enough fish to join the literati and become editors, columnists, presenters and, usually in a small way, writers. They think that being literary is a preliminary to writing good books, until time finds them out. But, after a while, it became evident that there was some difference between Edward and the others. He did not seem to seek precisely what they sought, or as they sought. He was not a great attender of literary parties, did little to cultivate influential people, and once turned down the chance to write a trial television script, an act of apparent self-neglect that scandalized his acquaintances. Without actually saying so, he gave the impression of an integrity that needed preserving, of having higher aims in view, though I see now that it might simply have been higher strategy. He began to be spoken of as someone rather special, as if he were already an authority, though no one asked on what.

Appearances helped, as nearly always. He was on the short side, well proportioned and with wavy blond hair that marked him out from one end of a street to the other. He had the regular good looks of the sort of male model who does summer casuals in open-top cars, usually by the sea or mountain lochs. There was a suggestion of ruggedness about him, almost of something soldier-like, but it was kept from crudity by the hint of contrivance. He had the posed nonchalance of the war correspondent rather than the matter-of-factness of the soldier. This self-consciousness added to his charm because you had the feeling that what was on offer was something he had made himself, especially for you. It was his mouth and eyes, however, that really captivated. His feminine lips were beautifully shaped, his smile small and almost shy, and his eyes startlingly blue. They spoke of seas and skies, of friendship, of layers and depths, while all the time giving the appearance of being fascinated by whoever engaged him. Such eyes are a great advantage because dark eyes are less suggestive of shades of meaning. A dark gaze always seems to have a more inward intensity, self-focused or sometimes simply dazzling, rather than one that steps out to meet you and makes you feel special. When I first knew Edward I used to practise before a mirror, trying to get my own brown eyes to step out and respond as his did. But whereas his seemed to project his whole being upon you, mine showed only a baffled striving.

I confess I played no part in Edward's literary world

and I probably had an exaggerated idea of his own place in it at that time. I taught English in a comprehensive school, an activity far removed from literary matters, and it pleased me to be able to say that I knew an author even if few had then heard of him. Apart from articles and reviews, he had at that time published nothing, though he had had a one-act play put on in the upstairs room of a pub. He worked away on his first novel but it seemed more likely that he would take the direct path into the literary establishment by seeking to become a literary editor on one of the major papers. These are the people with the widest powers of patronage, who sit on prize committees, decide how much review coverage a book gets, how much publicity its author is worth, get paid to talk on radio and television and become literary "figures." It helps to be known to be working on a book but its appearance should ideally be delayed for some years until the name is well enough known to ensure good sales. These are the people who decide, in part, what becomes literary fashion and what is merely stuff to fill the British Library.

I always thought Edward would become one of them, despite his seeming unwillingness to push himself. He was an incisive, quotable reviewer, personable, not short of ideas and looked right. Why he kept in touch with me while other university friends went adrift in his wake, I don't know. We had never been particularly close. Perhaps it was out of habit formed through our proximity in Kennington; perhaps he liked now and again to talk to someone from outside his new world, or perhaps he wanted a disciple.

Because I was certainly that. I was convinced he was on the threshold of great things and I felt privileged to know him. I dare say there was in the back of my mind some idea of myself as one of those who in later life are sought out by biographers and television interviewers. It didn't matter to me that it was a pretty one-sided friendship; that was just the way of it. Every three weeks or so I would ring him. He rarely rang me and only once, I think, came to my flat, which was when he wanted to borrow my car. I would go round to his place for coffee, whisky and talk. Occasionally we would go out for a curry or a pizza. Edward was a careless eater, indifferent to what he ate, a scavenger who didn't bother if he wasn't hungry and when he was would eat anything, anywhere, at any time. The fridge in his flat was almost always empty apart from a carton of milk for his tea and coffee, a few pieces of sliced bread still in their wrapper and a scrap of New Zealand butter that stayed exactly as it was, I believe, throughout his years alone. He scavenged for his food. I remember his saying once that he was a scavenger of ideas, too, but I don't recall whether that was before it all started.

Yet he was very tidy and the flat was almost eerily clean. It was in a tall terraced house with a forbidding exterior and gloomy, unkempt common parts. He was on the ground floor and his main room overlooked the street. He had his desk facing the window, which he claimed not to find distracting because so little went on in the quiet street. I used to wonder whether it was really so that he could save on electricity, which is what the reason would have been in my case. The room itself was not at all how I had expected a writer's room to be. Where one gets these ideas, I don't know, but I remember expecting to find it littered with old books and pipes—though Edward did not then smoke—and furnished with worn leather armchairs, a large old desk, an open fire, an old-fashioned standard-lamp and some bit of exotica such as a skull or a parrot. Instead of which, the room was clinically white with a fitted beige carpet and adjustable metal bookshelves filled with new books. It was furnished with one metal-framed upright armchair, a desk and chair of the modern office sort, a small filing cabinet, a flexible table-lamp and two radiators. The fireplace was covered and there were no paintings. I never knew Edward to show any interest in music—except during a brief late period but that was not for the sake of the music—nor in painting, and he was never in the least discomforted by lack of decoration. I like to clutter a room. I fill space wherever

I see it but he either didn't notice or used positively to relish the emptiness. No doubt that added to the impression it gave of being a cold room. It was a cold that had nothing to do with temperature. A kind of patient, calculated waiting.

It was in that room that it started, at least as far as I was concerned, although the origins were far away. I have tried to remember whether Edward gave any sign of having an inkling, whether he was, in fact, waiting; but I can recall nothing except one remark he made and that may have been coincidental. It was after he had turned down the television script and I had taxed him with neglect of his career. He swivelled in his typist's chair to face me and smiled his small smile. The light was behind him and half his face was in shadow.

"I don't think my career is something I need pursue," he said. "It's more a question of patience and recognition, of seizing the moment. Then it will pursue me."

That remained in my mind but it was only much later that I discovered I had remembered it. Edward had the reputation of being a brilliant talker yet he was far from voluble and I remember little of what he actually said. Others, I know, have found the same and it contributes to the increasingly unreal impression left by his career and reputation, an impression that affects even me. Conversely, I can always recall the exact timbre of his voice, the quiet and precise enunciation that lent such gravity to what he said that even when he used the same words as someone else they seemed to mean more. I don't know that he really was wittier than other people but the way he spoke made it seem so. It was as if he put his words in inverted commas and so detached himself from them, reserving his position. I would tell others of Edward's humour, yet I rarely laughed in his company, and he almost never in mine.

His remark about his career I interpreted as meaning that it was a question of seeing and seizing the moment in artistic terms. He published his first novel soon afterwards and I remember he spoke about it as the time drew near. Normally he adhered to the wise practice of never discussing work in progress but one evening he was more unbuttoned than usual and he described what he had tried and failed to do in the book. He was more self-critical than most writers and talked more of his failures; when, later, praise and prizes were bestowed upon him he would make only the odd remark such as, "It's not as good as they say," or, "It's not all it seems." But he talked at some length about that first book. He had, he said, tried to write a conscience-free novel; all novels involved the operation of conscience in one way or another and he had thought it ought to be possible to write one in which it played no part. Now, with the book about to be published, he had to admit that he had failed. He smiled as he said this and his smile had the curious effect of making the book seem immune to his own criticism, as if that particular failure were of little consequence. Conscience was implicit, he said, even in its lack, and that was why a conscience-free novel was as impossible as a conscience-free life. But he thought that other aspects of the book, notably its setting and story, were sufficiently strong for the real aim and failure to pass unnoticed. He was right. When it came out it was well reviewed and sales were above the norm for a first novel.

It was on that same night that he gave me a signed pre-publication copy. I was delighted, but I would have found literature in a street atlas if Edward had written it. In fact, it *is* a good book and has stood the test of time. It is fresh, tells a story, has a balanced perspective and an intelligent voice; in my opinion, it is also strengthened by the very lack of that style for which Edward was to become so famous. He used to say then that the best style is the least noticeable because it so directs the reader's attention to what is being written about that he is unaware of how the trick was done, or that there was a trick. I still believe that.

Anyway, the book was more than good enough for me. I did not then read contemporary novels with the searching thoroughness that I do now but I think it compared pretty well with its peers. I was also flattered that he talked to me about his work at such length and it made me feel for him an affection he would not often permit, no matter how ready I might have been to give it. But there was something else. After he had handed me the book I sat in the tubular chair, turning the pages, while he remained at his desk, half facing me, the light still behind him. It was probably for only a few seconds that neither of us spoke, but quite suddenly the silence became oppressive. It changed with the rapidity of focus in a film and the effect on me was like one of those terrifying dreams from which you cannot free yourself; you lie, conscious and impotent, beneath a great weight of fear, your soul—if that's what it is—fluttering like a stricken bird. I tried to speak and it seemed that for a long time I couldn't, though it may have been almost no time at all. Finally I said how quiet it was, and felt my heart thumping in my chest as if I had escaped something.

Edward replied without moving, "It's why I live here. I can work only in silence."

That was all. There was nothing to it. There still isn't, but I had cause to remember it later.

I did not go to Edward's publication party, though I was invited, because of Chantal. She was about the only reason in the world at that time that could have prevented me. She was the new French *assistante* at school and this was our first dinner. In fact, it was theatre followed by dinner. The play was one of those forgettable political message-bearers so beloved of the National Theatre at that time but it didn't matter because it gave us something neutral through which we could show off ourselves and explore each other over dinner. Naturally, I found a way of mentioning Edward's book and the publication party, not saying in so many words that I had turned it down for her but trying to let her know.

I daresay I overdid it because I was still speaking when she smiled and said, "You should have gone. We could have had dinner another night."

I had thought of that but having plotted for weeks to ask her out, then having screwed up the courage to do it and finally having been so surprised by her easy assent that I was stumped for what to say next, I did not want to hazard it all by changing now. I had fallen for her as I had never fallen for anyone else. She had fair hair and freckles—which she thought a blemish—and a smile which softened her features nearly to the point of blurring them. When she listened to someone talking her smile never quite left her. She had also the charm of difference; French women may or may not be intrinsically better-looking than British women but they see themselves differently, and so they often are. Probably something similar could be said about the men: their pride may often be comical but it gives them an alertness and an eagerness to please that makes them more attractive.

Chantal and I became engaged shortly before Edward published his fateful review of O. M. Tyrrel's last novel. If no longer at the height of his powers, Oliver Tyrrel was still riding the crest of his reputation. He was, of course, known to admirers and enemies alike as Old Man Tyrrel, or simply as the Old Man, and by his recent rejection of the Booker Prize he had demonstrated that his flair for publicity was undimmed by his eighty-five years. His marriages—which until the age of forty had outnumbered his novels—had become the subjects of books by embittered or greedy former spouses and he featured regularly in the colour supplements. His novels were translated into more than twenty languages and sold hugely. He lived in impenetrable privacy at Villefranche, between Antibes and Monte Carlo, and his domestic arrangements, involving a woman over half a century younger than himself, were often the subject of press interest. Headlines were sometimes made by his forays into politics, usually because of the bizarre or contradictory causes he chose, and it was hard not to suspect that that was why he chose them. He had opposed almost everything at one time or another and had thereby acquired in the eyes of many, including nervous governments, a surprising moral authority, as though his really was a standpoint of untouchable objectivity. Others regarded him as credulous, interfering and posturing.

What no one had publicly questioned, until Edward's review, was Tyrrel's literary reputation. He was the doyen of English letters. For decades he had squatted like a toad upon the summit of literary fashion, not suppressing new movements so much as rising with them, always on top. It was as if they could not be properly established until straddled by Tyrrel and this had gone on for so long that it seemed the natural order of things.

At the time of Edward's review it was not of course known that this book was to be Tyrrel's last, though there were signs that he was nearing the end. It was a tired book, possibly a re-working of old material, a book in which the driving idea was not sufficiently bodied forth in character and action and so showed through like the ribs of an old ship. The Old Man no longer had the energy or imagination to endow it with independent life, yet it remained of interest because in both theme and treatment it was similar to the novels of his youth, before he had become famous. His first book had been a very traditional novel about a man haunted by an act of betrayal committed many years before, and now in his last Tyrrel attempted a modern version of the Faust theme. But it was done too nakedly, and too late, in a way.

Edward's review was really more an article which dealt summarily with the book in question and then transferred its fire to the whole of Tyrrel's *oeuvre*. He was writing for one of the weeklies and so had more space than usual but even that meant only a dozen paragraphs. It was a masterly piece of succinct and reasoned assessment which read like a summing-up by a judge of indisputable wisdom and impartiality, and it was quite devastating. The essence was that Tyrrel had started his career well but then, in thrall to the idea of himself setting the fashion, he had retreated from reality and from any notion of duty to his art and had succumbed to the illusion that he somehow embodied that art. The consequence was a perpetual straining after novelty and an increasing "interiority" in his work. It was not his characters who mattered to him but his own reactions and thoughts; he assumed that they mattered equally to everyone else. It was as if nothing was real unless he had written it. This is not, of course, unknown among novelists and is only gradually fatal but Tyrrel, perhaps more perceptive than most, soon realized that his own thoughts were less sustaining and original than he might have liked and so he sought refuge in style. This was disguised self, this emphasis on style at the expense of everything, this insistence not only that matter and manner could be separated but that the one was more important than the other. In his most famous novels, said Edward, Tyrrel was little more than a fox chasing his tail; hoping by his antics to entrance his audience while all the time his books were about less and less. For all his fame, the great body of his work was really no more than a parody of what he might have done, a dance around emptiness.

As often with literary controversies, the effects of criticism were beneficial for all concerned. Discussion of Tyrrel's books further stimulated his sales, the weekly in which the review was published took a step nearer to establishing itself as a serious journal and Edward's name was made. In fact, what he had written was not actually controversial since nearly everyone agreed with it; the door was already ajar but none before him had thought to push it. Once he had, everyone else hurried through. Edward was immediately spoken of as if he were himself an established author, even a literary authority. His one novel was mentioned as if it were well known, which it then became. Yet it was not that he had said what no one before had thought; rather, he had said what they had all thought, if only they had realized it. He had arrived in one bound.

The most surprising consequence was the reaction of the Old Man himself. As famed for his refusal to discuss his books as for the secrecy of his personal relations, he nevertheless wrote asking if Edward would like to visit Villefranche and interview him "if you are not already weary of writing about me." Edward showed me the letter when I first took Chantal to his flat to introduce her. We were all three excited: me because I was with her and was introducing her to the man I thought of as my best, if not always my closest, friend; she because she was engaged and was meeting the youthfully famous author; he because of his letter.

He showed it to us with a smile, saying it would be typical of the Old Man only to have sent it when he knew he was dying and would be gone before Edward arrived. I remember noticing the tiny wavering signature which curled so far downwards at the end that the tail almost rejoined the body. I believe Hitler's did the same in his final years, the mark, perhaps, of a mind besieged. But there was something sinister, almost cabalistic, about this signature which made me stop smiling. It seemed to speak of an intense pressure, a little circle of unending pain, unreachable and inexpressible, utterly private. But the others did not seem perturbed and I looked at it no more.

We all went out for a curry. Chantal and Edward were each at their best and I was happy to see them. I really was very happy and proud. There had been talk of one of Edward's girlfriends—an imprecise and fluctuating group of women, one or two of whom I had briefly met—coming to join us but he said he hadn't got round to ringing any of them. As it was, the three of us formed a sort of bond that evening which lasted many years. We agreed we would all meet in France. Chantal and I were going to Antibes during the school holidays to stay with her family there, whom I had not met. With no pressing from me—I had thought of it but feared rejection, always finding his polite, quiet rejections more demoralizing than anyone else's—Edward volunteered to join us down there and "beard old Tyrrel," as he put it. Antibes would be a few miles along the coast from Tyrrel's house at Villefranche. We would all get together.

Insofar as happiness consists in a state of anticipation, that evening marked the high point of the last happy period of my life. I have known contentment since, and busy productive engagement, but anticipation has become an ever darker matter and the knowledge of what was put in train then has in any case undermined my belief in the possibility of anything unalloyed.

Chapter 2

❧ DECEMBER IN ANTIBES is often warm—shirt-sleeve weather, but cool enough for a jacket in the evening. The holiday-makers who make the place still more unbearable during the summer—it is already unbearably hot for my taste—have gone, leaving their yachts bobbing and twinkling in the harbour. The town recovers itself, shops and restaurants are open in sufficient numbers to make life comfortable, the covered fruit and vegetable market is bustling but uncrowded and in the bars there are shadows, dark corners and quiet talk. The town has a leisurely, post-prandial feel, conducive to everything and nothing.

Chantal's parents lived with their younger daughter, Catherine, in a modern apartment block overlooking the harbour. Their flat was big and expensive and most of the rooms had views of the sea, the old castle and the rocky coastline beyond. After the endless grey of a mild London winter, the blues and greens and whites and the wholly unexpected brightness made me feel twice as alive. Everywhere was flooded by a great radiant clear light. I could see the effect on Chantal. She seemed simpler, quicker, more natural, less considered. It did us both good to get away from the neurotic tedium of school and she was almost as excited as I was about Edward coming down. We talked about it to her family who, like most of the inhabitants of that coast, found it as natural that a famous foreign author such as Tyrrel should wish to live among them as it was unthinkable that they should read his books. They thought it equally natural that a friend of ours should be the only writer in thirty years to be invited to interview the great recluse, as if there were not many English writers and those there were had to make the best of each other. At Chantal's suggestion I rang Edward to invite him to stay but got only his answerphone. I guessed he had already left since he had spoken of spending a few days in Paris and then making his way south. I was secretly a little relieved because I suspected he would prefer his own arrangements and I didn't want him to turn us down.

One day, before he came, I went with Chantal to Villefranche. We had no particular aim other than the seeing of it and took the little train that runs along the coast at the backs of the houses and flats. It seems to me to be verging on the indecent to see houses from behind, with their washing, their untidy backyards, crumbling brickwork and stained concrete, as if one were getting an unsought view of people whose nether garments were tattered and soiled. I don't like to look and I tried to explain this to Chantal but it only made her laugh.

I was spared the rear view of Villefranche, however, because the station is cut into sheer rock and opens to the sea. It is a beautiful natural harbour, bounded on one side by the old town with its tall, tottering buildings, red roofs and white Roman and Saracen fort, and on the other by Cap Ferrat which curls round like a great protective arm and ends in a fist of rock and greenery. The Cap still has a generous covering of trees and foliage, albeit dotted much more numerously than before with the white walls of villas. Those down by the sea are palatial, those higher up smaller but more secluded. Even the new flats and hotels, built where the spur joins the coast, did not at that time greatly mar the curvaceous beauty of the place. It was no wonder that Tyrrel chose to live there but it was a wonder that he kept working. To me, it was a place in which I would die gazing, arrested in a lifelong dream.

We wandered through the narrow steep streets of the old town and along the tunnel of shops and doorways that had apparently been of much use to defenders during Saracen raids. In one small square a crew was filming two girls in fur coats getting into and out of a red car. It seemed they were advertising the car but I was more struck by the insouciant beauty of the two girls. One would not, I thought, see such in England, unless in London. Nor would one expect the insolent good looks and offhand charm of the director who talked, Gauloise dangling from his lips, with a series of morose Gallic shrugs and despairing, economical gestures. The girls looked languidly bored.

We found a place for lunch nearby, a narrow-fronted restaurant which looked like a bar and felt good the moment we stepped inside. The tables had plain white paper covers and the tiny bar, which served also as cheese-counter and cash-desk, was of old polished wood. The first room gave onto a smaller and darker inner chamber. Chantal, I think, would have stayed in the lighter room but I am always more fond of depths and recesses, so we went through. From it we could look back into the outer room and down the cobbled street to the harbour.

Coming from the brilliant light outside to the darkness of that little room, we did not at first realize that we were not alone. It was the smell of cigar smoke and a murmuring male voice that made us notice the tall elderly man with white hair who sat sideways on his chair, his back and head resting against the wall. He was with a much younger woman who had her back to us, her long black hair tied in a ponytail. Every so often she put her hand behind her head and flicked her hair free of the chair, upon which it kept catching when she leant back. When the man stopped speaking he re-lit his cigar, his thick fingers fumbling the matches. The woman said something and there was a pause. He spoke and there was another pause. It was as if some well-rehearsed and hopeless negotiation was being desultorily gone over yet again.

Chantal had her back to them both and it was only as my eyes adjusted to the gloom that I realized it was Tyrrel. The cigar, the sprawling white hair, the marvellously wrinkled face and the imperious profile were suddenly familiar from a score of Sunday papers, though they usually had no more of his words to report than I had then. When I told Chantal we both started to laugh. It seemed so absurdly natural, so unreasonably appropriate. It was the sign of providential approval of our holiday, an indication that the world really was adjusting itself to us. I looked forward to telling Edward.

At one moment our laughter at our luck—and at Villefranche, at Antibes, at all good lunches in all good restaurants, at being away from school and London, at ourselves—bubbled over, and Tyrrel's companion half turned towards us. I couldn't see her clearly but had the impression of a sharply attractive face, not the bored touch-me-if-you-dare beauty of the models with the car but a searching, intelligent quickness. We decided, of course, that she had to be Tyrrel's youthful, always unnamed mistress.

There was a commotion in the outer room, voices, laughter, the sounds of tables and chairs being moved, the popping of corks. It was the film crew, upon whose Gallic typicality I had just been expatiating; now I had to swallow my words with my wine because it was immediately apparent that they were all British. We laughed about this, too. Tyrrel turned towards the noise and I had a glimpse of his full face. It was old, sagging and lop-sided, scored and wrinkled like scorched leather. He was such an institution that it was easy to forget how old he was. But the face was alive and beneath his monstrously sprouting white eyebrows he had very blue eyes, like Edward's. He said something to the woman, who nodded and flicked her ponytail again. Shortly afterwards they left.

We did not stay long. One's compatriots are always an embarrassment abroad and the tones and clichés of Sloane Square or Wardour Street, or wherever they all hang out, were like repeated blows on the ear. Also, the sheer noise of all those squealed superlatives was deafening in that small place. It was a relief to close the door on them.

We wandered down to the harbour. Most of the town was shut during the early afternoon and the very sea seemed sleepy. I wanted to explore the fort but Chantal spotted Tyrrel and the woman walking slowly around the curve of the bay towards Cap Ferrat on the far side.

"That is where he actually lives," she said. "Shall we follow them? Then we can tell Edward how to get there."

There were not many people about and we kept well back. Tyrrel walked very slowly, the woman holding his arm. He was tall and leant towards her, his white head nodding, so that it looked from a distance as if she were supporting him. Perhaps she was. I was surprised that someone of his age should attempt that walk, let alone the climb at the end of it which became apparent when we reached the Cap. Long flights of concrete steps led up past large villas to a road junction. They kept stopping and so we had to do the same. At times it almost seemed as if she were forcing him on and during one of their rests he broke away from her, raising his arm. She let him go for a few steps, then caught up with him and took his arm. Each time they stopped we turned to admire the view. The azure sky, the calm twinkling sea, the old white buildings of the harbour, the greenery of the Cap as it beetled down far ahead of us, the three fishing boats drawn up on the beach of a tiny secondary harbour below and one tall old house that seemed to grow straight from the sea were all the stuff

of picture-postcards. Then we would turn again to follow the tall old man in brown corduroys and the
woman with bare brown legs, a long black ponytail and
a loose white skirt.

When we had reached the junction where the road
dips down to run along the bottom of the Cap we
found there was still more climbing. Tyrrel and the
woman had crossed the junction and were ascending a
path through grass and trees. This turned out to be the
narrow lane, the Chemin des Moulins, which runs
along the very spine of the Cap and feeds a number of
older cottages and unobtrusive villas. No vehicles can
get there, which is probably what has saved the area,
though to judge by the number of burglar alarms it was
no longer as private as it might once have been. We had
to close up on our quarry to see at which gate they
would turn. They were going ever slower.

"She'll kill him, making him climb like this," said
Chantal.

The Old Man had one arm round the woman's
shoulders and put his other hand on the gateposts as
he came to them. Twice they stopped for him to lean
against a hedge before eventually they turned in at a
small wooden gate. We let them get out of sight and
then ambled past. It was an old house and not, from
that side, very large, though as most of it faced across
the bay it was hard to judge. It had rough plaster walls,

28

small windows and large red curved tiles. A later extension had been added at one end, providing an extra storey which looked out across the water to Villefranche. The garden, which had been levelled in broad steps, was filled with olive trees and fell very steeply to the road below, out of sight. On the other side of the lane the ground dropped just as steeply in a tangle of olive trees and neglected garden. It might possibly also have belonged to Tyrrel since there was no other obvious claimant. Beyond it the coast curved in long lines of surf towards Monte Carlo. From the upper storey of the extension it must have been possible to view both sides of the Cap simultaneously.

We stood for a while looking at the two views until it grew colder and the sun was rapidly swallowed by a black cloud that sprang from beyond the Cap. The harbour changed from blue to indigo and the water became ominously smooth, moving like a carpet with the wind beneath it. I remembered that Tyrrel had written about the squalls that blow up out of nowhere on that coast at certain times of the year, how the sea may boil and blacken in a moment, devouring yachts and small craft as the wind knocks them flat upon the water.

"It's going to rain," said Chantal. "Come on."

She hated the rain, whereas I like it; it is stimulating and varied and has many moods. I particularly like the small warm rain of an English spring. But this was obviously going to be something different and so we hurried down some steps that ran alongside Tyrrel's garden to the road far below. There was no shelter on the lane but we thought there might be some on the road. After a few yards, I stopped and looked back. The part of the extension facing Villefranche had two large French windows, one above the other and divided by a balcony. In the upper window stood the woman. I was too far away to see her face clearly but again I had the impression of an almost ornithological sharpness. She reached slowly behind her head with both hands, her bare arms uplifted, and loosened her ponytail. She shook her head and spread her hair with her fingers, her eyes all the time on the heavy smooth sea and the black cloud that now covered the harbour. In the room below stood Tyrrel, his hands in the pockets of his corduroys, his shoulders slumped. Like her, he stared at the apocalyptic darkening.

There were some improbably large drops of rain. Chantal called. She was standing at an angle in the steps by a broken-down old shed. I was about to join her when there was a sky-wide flash of lightning. The harbour was now the deepest indigo and heaved as if in labour. The churning clouds thickened and blackened and the old fort on the tip of Villefranche stood out against sea and sky with an unreal whiteness. There was more lightning, followed by thunder, and more raindrops, heavier and faster.

In the upper room the woman again stretched her arms above her head, looking along each arm at her outspread finger-tips, turning her hands forward and back. She then turned right round, her arms still raised, and walked to the back of the room, disappearing as if into an embrace. Below her the Old Man stood, morosely staring, but as the thunder rolled again and the rain began in earnest he raised his hands to his face.

Chapter 3

❦ THAT OCCASION was the nearest Chantal and I came to a row before we married. She sheltered in the shed but the corrugated iron roof leaked and made her hair wet. I did not come the moment she called and that annoyed her, even though she would have been no drier if I had and it was me who got soaked running the ten yards from where I had been standing. The rain came at a bewildering variety of angles and with a seemingly personal ferocity. It stung my cheeks and head and all but blotted out the house. The old comparison with stair-rods did not seem such an exaggeration. But I was laughing, which irritated her, and I was keen to tell her about what I had seen, which further irritated her. The surface of our relationship was broken by a deep exasperation which I had not seen before. It was as if the sea, when it was calm and bright, had shown for an instant a glimpse of something sinister.

"Don't be stupid," she said, emphasizing the last word.

It was only a moment and soon she was scolding me for being wet in a manner that anticipated her capacity for prompt and opinionated motherhood, a quality which in those days I found charming. I relished the attention.

Edward arrived not long afterwards. He rang and said he had booked into a small hotel in Antibes, having been unable to find anywhere both open and available in Villefranche. Tyrrel had not asked him to stay. He was slightly reluctant to meet before seeing Tyrrel but I told him we had something important to tell him and so we all three had dinner on his first night at M. Englert's, down by the old harbour. Out of season Englert's is a restful place in which you can sit all day over your coffee with a paper or a book. If I were a writer I would work in places like that, taking a table in a window so that I could watch the world go by, private, unmolested, unseeing when I didn't want, but plenty to watch when I did.

Over dinner that night we all three had the kind of conversation that made Chantal and me realize there was something we missed about London after all, only we had not known until we tasted it again. Edward wore a blazer and tie, rather more formal than his usual dress but it soon ceased to seem out of place and by the end of the evening it felt as if he were the host and we the strangers. His French was good—better than mine—and it came out that he had spent most of his school holidays with French relatives in Chantilly. That was the first time it struck me how little I knew of his background. He came from Yorkshire where his father was a solicitor—his mother too, I think, though they were divorced—and he had a brother and sister of whom he saw little. Most people refer quite often to their past but Edward hardly ever did. Indeed, he referred very little to himself at all. He would talk about what was going on, about books or about people and he would always question whomever he was with, getting them to talk. In this way he gave the impression of being communicative while in fact keeping himself in reserve. There was also something about him that discouraged questions; the impression that things which may have been important to others were, when it came to him, too trivial to bother with. It was as if he were hardly interested in the accidents of history and personality but only in his purpose, which could never be discussed in any detail without breaching the work-in-progress rule.

When we came to relate our encounter with Tyrrel it seemed rather thinner than it had at the time. We must have made it sound as if we were building up to an exchange of words or perhaps even a message, whereas there was only my description of what I had seen in the rain. I was repetitive and laboured it more than I should have, to the point where hyperbole threatened coherence. Edward's blue eyes and regular features attended without a flicker, which I found more disconcerting than if he had shown signs of restlessness and embarrassment, like Chantal. I ended by urging him to see Tyrrel before he died of a heart attack or did away with himself. He said they were to meet the following night and, perhaps as a kindness, suggested the three of us meet again in Englert's the night after.

I shall not relate all of what follows in the sequence in which it revealed itself to me. If I did, you would read in the very fog in which I myself lived for so many years. There must be many of us who think we know where we are and are sure about what we see before us, until people or events prove us wrong, as they not uncommonly do. When that happens to other people one can view it with equanimity; when it happens to you it feels uniquely invidious and unfair, almost an outrage, perhaps as dying might feel. And even now, looking back on it, I know I cannot see everything.

On the morning after Edward had seen Tyrrel—therefore, on the day on which we were to dine again—it was announced that Tyrrel had died during the night. Perhaps it was an omen that Chantal and I went all that day without knowing, albeit an omen with more reference to me than to her. It is one of the features of our world that we may receive news of events in other continents virtually simultaneously with their occurrence while our neighbour's death on the other side of the bathroom wall may happen unnoticed. Not, of course, that Tyrrel was a neighbour but his death only a few miles along the coast was an international event of which we knew nothing because we did not bother with television or radio that day and because those that did had no pleasure in passing on news which they assumed everyone else to know. Thus are we deprived of the daily discovery and discussion of events which must in the past have contributed so much to local self-importance. Whatever the reason, Chantal and I wandered about all day without anyone thinking to mention Tyrrel.

It was only when we were about to go and meet Edward that Catherine, Chantal's younger sister, said: "You were lucky to see that English author. I wonder if he died when your friend was with him."

We hurried to M. Englert's and waited but Edward didn't come. We said we were sure he would have rung if he couldn't make it and then, because we weren't, I telephoned the hotel. They said there was no answer from his extension. I was all for going round and seeing but Chantal sensibly insisted we eat first. Next I was seized with an irrational fear that Edward was somehow responsible for Tyrrel's death and was even now being accused of murder. Chantal nearly choked with laughter. Why, she asked, did I suspect Edward of doing violence? He seemed the most calm, the most polite and peaceable of men. What I couldn't explain was that it wasn't so much the likelihood or otherwise of Edward's killing Tyrrel that concerned me—it is curious that I took it for granted that he was capable of it—so much as the feeling that something had happened to him.

We did go to his hotel after dinner but there was no answer from his room. I suggested to Chantal that we borrow her father's car and drive along to Cap Ferrat. She was incredulous: why was I so worried? Edward was not a child, he knew how to pick up the telephone if he needed help. And Tyrrel was dead, so what point was there in staring at his house in the dark? She had never seen me like this, she said; I was worse than a worried parent, stupid (she used that word again). Nevertheless I persisted and we did borrow the car, having checked that Edward had not telephoned.

It was a quiet night and it did not take long to drive to Cap Ferrat. I thought Chantal was going to be irritated with me again but she seemed resignedly amused, or perhaps just resigned. There was a heavy sprinkling of stars and from the road that ran along the bottom of Cap Ferrat the moon laid a rippled path across the bay to the fort. We stopped by the steps we had come down during the squall.

"I'll wait here," said Chantal.

The absurdity of what I was doing struck me as I climbed the steps alone. To be more accurate, I was struck by how absurd I must appear but I didn't feel absurd at all. I felt that I was doing what had to be done though I couldn't have said why. I am not psychic; at least, no more so than most people. I have no talent for telepathy or anything like that and no particular beliefs. Throughout this account I am trying to record what happened, or appeared to happen, because it may be happening still. But after all these years I cannot always be clear as to what *did* happen, especially as it was not clear at the time. Contrary to what is often said, the everyday language we use for describing what happens to us is quite well suited to its purpose; it is—or can be made to be—precise. It is much more difficult to describe the half-world in which things half-happen, in which something may become visible only when it is looked for, audible only when listened for, present only when expected. Nor is it enough to write off such half-things as the products of a single credulous mind since by chance or design they often impinge upon others. There are, I believe, stranger phenomena known to physics: sub-atomic particles occupying no space but having velocity and direction and a pattern of behaviour that is modified by the mere fact of being observed.

I felt rather like one myself that night. The steps were uneven and overhung by bushes but eventually I found the place above the shed where I had stood in the rain. There were one or two lights in the house but none in the windows where I had watched Tyrrel and the woman, though the moon was bright enough for me to see a little way into those rooms. I stood for some time, nonplussed. I don't know what I had expected but I had expected something, and now there was nothing. I felt disappointed and frustrated, even cheated. I stared stubbornly at the big empty windows. A creature rustled in the grass nearby and a breeze stirred the olive trees. I was conscious of keeping Chantal waiting below but still I stared. I felt drawn towards the windows and it occurred to me that I hadn't yet got to where I was going. A few steps farther up there was a gap in the fence where palings had come away and were hanging askew. I ducked through into the long grass and tangled undergrowth. It sounded to my own ears that I was making a great deal of noise. I realized that the house might well be occupied, that I might be arrested in such a thief-conscious neighbourhood and that no explanation I could give would be at all credible; but I pressed on through the undergrowth until I stood in a clear area about twenty yards down from the house and in front of the two windows. I did not worry about the moonlight.

I will not say definitely that I saw something, though I think I did. What I do assert, even after all these years, is that I had the most vivid impression that I was being seen. The anxiety I had felt all evening and that had brought me there in the absence of any good reason, evaporated. I felt that this was what I had come for, as if I had been summoned. I was neither frightened nor particularly excited and I no longer thought of Edward. I continued to stare at the windows but calmly, without urgency now, and it was after a while of this that I thought I saw the woman again. She was standing in the upper window looking down at me. I say "thought" because I wasn't sure even then whether I was actually seeing her or simply experiencing a very strong impression of her. Not that it mattered; even a moment afterwards I could not have described her features. I could only have said that I felt I was held in a sharp, interrogative gaze.

It may have been some trick of the moonlight and perhaps that would be the sensible thing to believe. Yet there was a definite moment when it finished and it seemed to me that she turned away. My last image was of bare arms at first folded, and then raised as she turned, again as if into an embrace. I probably imagined the figure of a man behind her, deep in the room. After that there was no more and I no longer felt any reason to be there. I picked my way back through the undergrowth to the gap in the fence and walked slowly down the steps to Chantal and the car. When she asked me if I had seen anything I said I had not.

I was no longer anxious about Edward and when I saw him late the next morning sitting in the window of M. Englert's, as I was on my way back from the market, I was not even surprised. He sat with a cup of coffee and a cigar, pen and paper beside him. I had never seen him smoke before.

We greeted each other with a handshake, something we never did in England. I saw he had been doodling on the paper, large circular shapes with much interweaving.

"I was expecting you," he said.

His manner seemed to obviate questions as to why he had neither telephoned nor turned up the night before. It was as if his presence excused everything.

I sat down. "I've never seen you smoke."

He put the cigar to his lips and shrugged, his elbows on the table. His shirt was open at the neck, his sleeves were rolled up and he had not shaved that morning.

"What happened?" I asked, slightly irritated.

"We had good dinner and good talk. He had a heart attack after I left. He was found in the morning."

"I had a mad idea that you'd be implicated somehow and that the police would blame you."

"I had to make a statement. I was the last to see him."

"What about his woman?"

"Apart from her."

"What's she like?"

"She was hardly there. It was him and me."

"Him and me," with its suggestion of gladiatorial combat, seemed to have been the theme of the evening. From what Edward told me then it sounded as if he had triumphed in a struggle that had nevertheless enhanced his respect for his opponent. The rest I learned years later under very different circumstances, by which time it was clear that neither the struggle nor the result had been what he thought.

Edward told me that morning that the first thing that had struck him about Tyrrel was the Old Man's age, for which, like me, he had been unprepared. Tyrrel's literary fecundity and the attention that was paid to him made one think of him as a much younger man, but his spine was curved into a stoop, his movements were slow and uncertain, his hands knobbled and stiff and his blue eyes—that evening, anyway—

were rheumy. Yet his mind was more than sharp enough, as Edward was to discover, though at the time Edward's reaction was to feel guilty at having attacked so frail an old man, even in print. Whisky helped dispel the guilt. They sat in Tyrrel's study—the room in which I had seen him—which Edward described as bare and uncluttered, making it sound like his own. Tyrrel congratulated him on the review.

"I would not say you hit the nail on the head," Tyrrel said, "but you knocked it a good way in. Nonetheless, the lid is not quite down. There are more nails."

"I wasn't meaning to bury you."

The Old Man smiled. "The fox chasing its tail is a good analogy of the way I have frequently written. Style itself becomes the end and people forget to ask what it is for. You cannot entirely blame them. There is trickery in all art and if no one complains that a book is more trickery than substance there must be art enough in the trickery, which then becomes admirable. But what you said about my last book was wrong. You mishit that nail."

This was the novel based on the Faust theme that Edward's review was ostensibly about. It was, as I think I have said, less artistic and self-conscious than its predecessors, little more than a statement of its theme, a dramatic but bald assertion that in the end a price is paid.

"The simplicity of that book," said Tyrrel, "is deliberate. It is not due to lack of art or energy. It reflects the reality it describes. It is neither an aberration nor a throw-back but a confirmation of the unity of all my work. In the beginning was the bargain, then the years of success and elaboration, now the price." He smiled and poured more whisky. "I read your own novel after I had seen your review. It shows great promise and I believe it is the sign I have been seeking among young writers for many years now. It is, of course, a failure"— his rheumy eyes twinkled faintly—"but an interesting one. You tried to keep spirit out, did you not? Perhaps you didn't call it that but that's what it amounts to. You failed. But never mind. You must try again and keep trying. Look at my books, particularly the ones you think most foxily fraudulent. You will find it hard to write with less of the spirit than that; but you will try."

Tyrrel's speech was old-fashioned and clipped, more formal than ours. He spoke precisely in measured periods and his voice seemed younger than his body. His manner was courteous and he listened with attention. Yet Edward did not like him. He disliked the way in which, whatever they discussed, the Old Man seemed to want it both ways: yes, there was too much mere style in what he had written but that was deliberate, so it was all right; yes, his first and last books were stark

44

statements of theme but the theme itself was stark, so that too was all right; on the one hand, he was a writer who was political and on the other he was a political who wrote; he had always been of the Left, of course, though he had right-wing sympathies; he was utterly committed to his writing and could imagine no other life; at the same time, he was a writer who was prepared to commit himself to anything while being essentially committed to nothing. Of religion he said:

"Sympathize with all, believe nothing. And remember that the devil never lies."

There was something beneath Tyrrel's courtesy that Edward particularly disliked, a reserve, a coldness, a perhaps unreachable pride that deterred any real fellow-feeling. As Edward described all this in unusual detail it occurred to me that the same might be said of him, though I realized it intellectually without actually feeling it. I also thought that his conversation with Tyrrel did not sound as confrontational as he had said; more a laying-on of hands than a contest, I suggested.

Edward was curtly eager to convince me otherwise. "I haven't told you all. There was more to it than that." They had argued about matter and form, about substance and art, about *ex post facto* justification, about sincerity.

"Do you believe in sincerity?" Tyrrel had asked.

Like most of us, Edward assumed the answer to be so obvious that he had never asked himself the question. "Yes."

Tyrrel's smile was mocking. "I have a soft spot for romanticism."

"Sincerity pre-dates romanticism."

"Infinitely, infinitely."

I was still not clear why Edward regarded this as a victory.

Afterwards they ate pizzas which Tyrrel heated in a microwave oven. They discussed writing routines, a subject which I believe writers find more interesting than themes or theories. Tyrrel wrote in longhand on plain paper, with a fountain pen.

"Not even a typewriter?"

"I used to, years ago. Then I tried a word processor. But I gave them both up. I hear better with a pen in my hand."

"You hear the voices?"

"I hear the pen. It took a long time to accept that that is really my only choice, listening to the pen. I used to do anything I could to drown it but nothing ever worked. I had to surrender myself to it."

Edward assumed that this was no more than a pardonably eccentric way of saying that machines get in the way. He told me that it was after midnight—and a lot more whisky—when he left.

I assumed that Tyrrel's death meant that Edward's interview would be given sensational treatment—the Old Man's last words, his confrontation with his critic, his valedictory on literature and so on. Had he recorded it? I asked Edward.

He was staring out of the window at two girls in white who were talking by the steps that led up to the old town wall. "No, I didn't," he said absently. "I could've but I changed my mind. I didn't think he'd like it. It was more a conversation than an interview. More an exchange."

"But he'd invited you to do it. He must have expected you to write about him."

"I think the interview was a pretext."

"For what?"

He continued to stare at the girls by the steps and I thought he wasn't going to answer. "He wanted to talk."

"But it's such a good opportunity for you, after all you said about him. You'd get international coverage. You'd be made."

He shook his head.

I did not mention my escapade in the garden. At half-past eleven in the morning of a bright breezy day, over coffee and with my bag of vegetables on the seat beside me, it seemed as unreal and silly as it had to Chantal at the time. There was more, much more, that

Edward did not tell me then. He called it a postscript but he had always had a taste for understatement. What he said years later, when events had again moved him to a rare loquacity, was that as Tyrrel talked that night he had found it increasingly difficult to know what the Old Man was talking about. Nothing was demanded of Edward other than the semblance of mute attention and he found himself thinking that Tyrrel's talk was like so many of his books, a beguiling dance around nothing. At the same time he was reminded of what he himself had said about the last book, about the starkness of the theme showing through the skin. In this case, the theme was Tyrrel, a relentless, raging egotism, an invincible vanity that meant that every idea, every subject, every word came reeking with the stench of self. Those were Edward's words. Tyrrel talked about nothing for itself, nothing had significance except as it pertained to him. Edward let himself be carried along. It didn't seem to matter that he didn't attend since everything led back to Tyrrel. It was not an unpleasant process, rather the reverse. He had only to pay no heed to what words meant to feel that he was being borne along by a swift smooth current. At one point he did wonder if it was the whisky; it could have been that as well, of course.

The other sensation that came upon him was that they were approaching a climax. He sensed from

Tyrrel's manner and appearance that something was coming. The Old Man's eyes were brighter, his clipped speech was quicker and he seemed, for a while, younger.

Eventually, he said to Edward: "All my books have been taken from one text, you know, from one great manuscript that contains them."

"You mean you'd written them before?"

"No, but they pre-exist."

"A writer's notebook?"

The glitter in the Old Man's eyes was subdued. "Not a notebook but a text, a blueprint, a sort of literary genetic code."

"You wrote all this years ago and you've been drawing on it ever since?"

"It is very old. I have never told anyone else about it."

"It's nothing to be ashamed of."

"Would you like to see it?"

"Well—yes." Edward felt uneasy, as if there was something sinister in progress. Yet when he looked at the frail, stooping old man he felt ashamed of himself.

"It doesn't hurt," said Tyrrel, perhaps sensing Edward's reactions, "so long as you go along with it."

He got slowly to his feet and shuffled over to his desk drawer. At that moment he no longer looked younger but seemed every day of his eighty-five years. He put one trembling hand on the desk to support himself while with the other he tried to pull open the drawer. Edward offered to help.

"No!" Tyrrel's voice was startlingly gruff, filling the room. He opened the drawer an inch at a time. Then, moving as in slow motion, he reached in with both hands and withdrew the manuscript. It was not as bulky as Edward had thought and it was bound in yellowing string. The edges were tattered and the paper looked old and unusually thick. If what Tyrrel had said was true, he had taken over twenty books from it. It did not look big enough.

Tyrrel held the manuscript close to his chest, breathing heavily.

"Come here," he said. His voice was again gruff and though he faced Edward across the desk he did not look up.

Edward approached. There were drops—tears or sweat—on Tyrrel's cheeks. When Tyrrel did look up he was paler than before and his watery eyes were blank as if unfocused, or focused inwardly. He held out the manuscript.

"Take it," he whispered. His big hands shook and Edward was sure now that it was sweat running down his cheeks. He prodded Edward with the manuscript. "You must take it."

Edward did not move. He was disconcerted and unaccountably weary. A heaviness of spirit seemed to have dropped upon him and he either imagined or actually said, "I want to go home." He thought he heard the words but they were as if from outside himself.

The Old Man's skin was almost grey now and his wet cheeks quivered. He continued to stare at Edward but Edward had the impression that he was actually seeing something else. Edward was too concerned with himself to ask whether Tyrrel felt ill. The deadening sluggishness that had fallen upon him had reached his limbs. It was as if his very blood were heavy. At the same time he felt the point of a sharp, fierce eagerness, an urge to go on whatever the consequences. He did nothing.

Tyrrel spoke again. The words sounded like, "It is for you," or, "It is meant for you." Edward couldn't be sure because the voice was less than a whisper. They were the last words Tyrrel spoke.

Edward took hold of the manuscript. For a moment Tyrrel did not let go. His knobbled hands held strongly despite their trembling and he stared into Edward's eyes with the same bleak unfocused intensity. It was as if Edward were receiving some sort of sacrament. Then Tyrrel's grip weakened and he began to sway backwards. His still-living eyes were filled with horror. They filled as from behind like sea in a ship's porthole, complete and blank. "Horror" was an inadequate word,

Edward said, but there was no other; it was simply that. At the time he thought it was because Tyrrel was reading his mind since even as the Old Man fell, Edward's thought was that the manuscript was now his and that he could plagiarize it without anyone knowing. I do not know whether that was an unusual reaction, but I suspect many writers would have had it even if they did not act upon it. He also thought that that was why Tyrrel's hands gripped the manuscript with such tenacity, relinquishing it only in his last moment.

He was a big man and fell loudly, knocking over the chair and banging his head upon the wall. Sprawled on his back, he looked even bigger than when upright. One shoulder was against the wall and his head hung twisted on the other like a chicken's when its neck is broken. Years later Edward still remarked on the size of Tyrrel's upturned feet. They must have been at least twelves, he thought. He stared at the body for some time, holding the manuscript close to his chest, as Tyrrel had. He felt no pity, and it occurred to him neither to seek help nor to confirm that Tyrrel was past it. Instead, he felt a deep and secret exhilaration. It was as if he were suddenly free after years of servitude.

"So you left without seeing the woman?" I remember asking him.

"She was at the other end of the house."

Before leaving Tyrrel's study he closed the drawer.

He did not want the rest of the world to know about the manuscript and he preferred people to assume that Tyrrel had died after he left. So they did; he was able to satisfy the police that he had not been there at the time of death and the autopsy confirmed that Tyrrel had died of natural causes. Edward left the room with only the manuscript and the memory of the horror in Tyrrel's dying eyes. He felt, he told me later, as if the stare were still upon him.

I believe I am the only person other than those intimately involved ever to have seen that manuscript. Edward showed it to me. It is handwritten in faded brown ink on old laid paper. The writing is small and dense and the longer strokes very thin. It is in English and the individual letters are clearly formed and recognizable, yet of the whole I could make no sense; I could not read it. Admittedly, it was in my hands for only a few seconds and it may be that I simply wasn't concentrating, but I don't think so because Edward's early reactions were like mine. Those thousands upon thousands of thin spiky strokes gave me an uncomfortable sensation of nonsense, pernicious nonsense that was nevertheless tempting because at the same time it seemed that it could be made to mean something. And so it did for Edward; but it may be that you have to have the ambition to be a great writer before it will speak to you.

Chapter 4

As I HAVE SAID, it was years before I knew of the manuscript and that early time in London passed rapidly. Much of life is just one thing after another and it is hard to form any sort of reliable perspective. Yet this attempt to recall what became, without my realizing it, the great theme of my life forces me to adopt one, however rough and ready. In those early years Chantal and I married, worked, saw family and friends, read newspapers and books, went to theatres and cinemas, had holidays, moved up a rung or two of the property ladder and generally led that busy metropolitan life that seemed at the time so urgent and full and is now so largely forgotten.

Edward prospered. Not only did he write a lot but he struck a seam that was ready to be mined, at least by those concerned with literary fashion. He became a leading writer among what were then known as the post-modernists, exponents of something called "fictive realism" according to which reality and fantasy had the same status. This resulted in writers thinking that they could write what they liked, that they had no obligation to convince or render, that they need not discriminate except on grounds of what pleased them. The cause of this was a failure of imagination, or of belief in the power of imagination to interpret life, and it led to contempt for the reader. It had, I think, an intellectual justification at the time, a supposedly absolute scepticism which maintained that since reality was no more to be trusted than fantasy nothing could be finally proved—whatever that meant. Naturally, the writers and critics who believed this could do so only by walling themselves in behind a new absolute greater than any they claimed to attack, which was their sense of their own rightness. Their scepticism did not extend that far.

You may think that I was opposed to this movement, but far from it. It was only later that I came to see it as a betrayal and to believe that truth in art matters, that part of the role of art is to help us to hear what cannot usually be heard amidst all the noisy nonsense in which we live. I know I am old-fashioned—I who was so keen to be contemporary—but I have been made so by experience. It was the new truths that failed me, not the old ones, and I do now believe that anything that confuses reality and unreality, or that attempts to equate the two, is the devil's own work.

At the time, though, I was all for everything new. Flattered by Edward's friendship, I talked isms over drinks in Clapham gardens on Sundays, read what the reviews said I should, saw the plays and films that other people saw, thought what they thought, went eagerly to dinner parties. I was the very type of the modern philistine. To her credit, I think that for Chantal the whole business was more an act than it was for me; she wasn't taken in, and anyway posing came more naturally to her. She simply enjoyed it, whereas I thought it mattered. Perhaps I was already a little dull.

Though a leading exponent of the new writing, Edward was not a theoretician. In fact, I don't think I ever heard him espouse any particular theory. He simply put them into practice and during any discussion of theory, or even of other contemporary writers, he would smile and shake his head as if it were all above him, which gave the impression that it was in fact all below him. He kept his flat in that gloomy Kennington house even when he lived mainly abroad and could have bought the whole street. At one stage he owned a house in Chelsea as well and used the flat as a hideaway for work since in Chelsea he was besieged by telephone calls or business. But in those early years he continued to live there and I continued to call round, as before I was married. Sometimes Chantal would come but more often we were alone, unless one of his girlfriends was there. He was pretty ruthless about getting them out of the way but they became more a feature of his life than they had been. In fact, after those few days in Villefranche he became busier in every department of his life: he wrote more, saw more people, did more reviewing, sampled more women, appeared more often on radio and television and so became a national figure, at least so far as those who make a profession of the arts were concerned. I used to think that anyone who wrote much would have correspondingly less time for everything else, and once said so.

"No," he said, with a decisive shake of the head. "When the writing goes well, everything else goes well."

What puzzled me more was that his succession of women continued after Eudoxie had moved in. It may even have increased. But there was more than that that was puzzling about Eudoxie.

I met her the night I first heard the writing. I had no idea she was living with him—he had never mentioned her—and I had called round to ask him to sign a copy of his second novel, which I was giving to a friend. It had won one of the minor literary prizes and was, I think, the book that first prompted comparisons between Edward and Tyrrel. These were made not so much on grounds of literary similarity as in terms of their gifts for trendsetting; Edward was already showing signs of being ahead of the game. There were important differences in approach but the results were curiously alike. Whereas Tyrrel had first attracted attention by his style and had then refined his subject-matter almost to nothing so that towards the end, with the exception of his last book, an ever-more extravagant style was virtually all there was, Edward paid little apparent attention to style but advanced himself under cover of an artillery barrage of ideas, scenes, characters and caricatures. He mixed the real with the surreal and fact with fantasy in successive salvoes of such intensity and energy that the reader had no time to recover and discriminate. He wrote with a zest and wit that bamboozled judgement to the extent that critics no longer looked coolly at what was being said but let themselves be overwhelmed by the saying of it, just as with Tyrrel. When one or two started to talk of him as succeeding to the place in contemporary letters vacated by Tyrrel the rest joined in and soon they were competing with each other in the extravagance of their claims.

Edward took a rather wry attitude towards it all, appearing neither to endorse nor to disclaim. I even found myself telling people that success had not changed him and in some ways I was right: he lived and worked in the same place, I visited as before, our friendship seemed unaltered. Perhaps that was because it had always been less deep than I used fondly to think, no more than an occasional acquaintance so far as Edward was concerned, though there were other elements later. Certainly, that night I took the book for signing all appeared as usual. We talked over coffee and I gave him the book. He had met the friend it was for and so said he would add an inscription of his own.

I sat in the tubular-framed chair and Edward sat at his desk, his swivel chair turned side-on and his pen above the open book. He had paused while thinking what to say and my eye wandered round the white walls and the shelves of shiny books. I never could get used to the room being so antiseptic, so lacking in human warmth. I heard the scratching of pen on paper and looked back at Edward. His pen was motionless an inch or two above the open page yet the scratching continued. I looked around the room for some other source of noise but it was impossible to believe it was anything else. It had the rhythm of someone writing rapidly and regularly; I could tell long and short words and punctuation marks. The paper sounded coarse and the nib cruder than a modern one, like the sort you used to have to dip in the ink, or like a quill. The silence that always inhabited the room served to emphasize the thin, unremitting scratching.

Edward remained immobile, his pen still poised above his own open book. He held the page flat with his left hand and on his face was an expression of abstracted absorption. It made him look extraordinarily young, his cheeks smooth and boyish. It reminded me of Chantal when I had observed her playing the piano in her parents' flat. She was not an experienced pianist and she had not known she was being observed; her face had shown an intense listening vacancy, remote, unselfconscious, like Edward's now. When she saw me she was for a moment lost and confused, then irritated, finally briskly dismissive of her efforts.

"What's that noise?" I asked Edward.

He started as if someone had slapped his face and for a moment seemed not to know where the question had come from. "What noise?"

My impulse was to apologize but I felt suddenly guilty and I wanted to justify myself. "That scratching. I could hear someone writing and I thought it was you but you weren't moving."

He stared at me. "You heard it?"

"Yes. Pen on paper. I'm sure that's what it was."

"How long for?"

"The last minute or two. Since you've been thinking what to write."

"Can you hear it now?"

"No."

He looked down. "It only happens when I'm thinking." He quickly wrote an inscription in the book and handed it back.

"But what do you think it is?" I persisted.

He stared at me in a way that made me feel uneasy, as if he were someone assessing my future without any reference to myself. The blue of his eyes so enhanced their expressiveness that it took very little to make them intimidating. "Have you eaten?" he asked.

I had not; Chantal was out that evening and I had been going to get fish and chips.

"Eat here," he said. "There's something in the oven."

He got up and led the way down the hall to the kitchen. I had never eaten anything cooked at Edward's. Indeed, I had never known him to use his oven; he simply did not cook. I was so surprised that I gave up my pursuit of the scratching.

In the kitchen was a woman. My reaction must have been obvious because I remember I stopped in the doorway long enough for Edward to look round and say, rather peremptorily, "Come in, come in."

She was shorter than I remembered but there was no mistaking the dark hair, dark eyes and sharp, quizzical beauty. Her hair was in a ponytail, as in the restaurant with Tyrrel that day, and it emphasized the slightly Asiatic shape of her cheekbones and eyes.

"This is Eudoxie," said Edward.

We shook hands. I assumed from her accent that she was French, and said so.

"Partly, *un peu*. A little of everything." She wore dark red lipstick and when she smiled her teeth showed very white and even, packed closely together.

"He's having dinner with us," Edward said curtly.

She smiled again and began to busy herself around the stove while Edward and I sat at either end of the small table. She poured us each a glass of red wine and left the bottle between us, having waited like a waitress for Edward to taste. That seemed to be her role and even when she joined us for dinner she said little. I was fascinated; there was something wonderfully cosmetic about her and watching her face had the same fascination as watching a fire, the same flickering continuity and inconstancy, unchanging change. I was also fascinated by the way she and Edward were with each other. It was not only that she didn't look convincing playing the part of Oriental wife or waitress but that she and Edward gave the impression of having been a long time together. They were relaxed and familiar—"familiar" was a word that occurred to me time and again with regard to Eudoxie—as if long past the stage of tiptoeing around each other that most couples go through.

Over dinner, which was chicken with garlic, onions, olives and rice, Edward and I talked books. Eudoxie ate in silence except for one interlude. I had mentioned

J. P. Curran, a novelist even less known now than then, who had also met Tyrrel. I can't remember how I came to bring him up but I suspect I was so conscious of Eudoxie's connection with Tyrrel and felt so awkward about mentioning it directly that I kept stumbling upon references to the Old Man. I must have mentioned him half a dozen times during that meal. Anyway, the sad story of Curran is that he wrote a brilliant first novel as a result of which he was invited to stay with Tyrrel, something as unheard of as Tyrrel's invitation to Edward. Perhaps Tyrrel had seen Curran as an acolyte. Anyway, something went wrong and Curran left early. He left no account of his visit but was said to be writing a novel based on Tyrrel at the time of his premature death in Lincoln; the manuscript was never found.

I had said what a loss this was and Edward said he had never read Curran's book. Eudoxie raised a delicate forkful to her lips and shrugged.

"It was his own fault," she said. "He had his chance but did not take it."

I asked what she meant.

"He could have written much more but he didn't accept what was offered."

Her manner was remarkably unsympathetic. I felt as if I had said something which, however inoffensive to my ear, was to hers contentious. I tried to ameliorate.

"Well, it's a pity we can never now have the books he would have written."

"Of course we can," she said sharply. "Books are as inevitable as writers. They come when the time is right for them. The books Curran could have written will be written by someone else."

This bizarre idea she asserted with such confidence that I did not argue. I had heard Edward talk of books as "pre-existing," as waiting to be written, of authors as midwives, but I had assumed he was talking metaphorically. Eudoxie spoke with the literal-minded confidence of the stupid, but I couldn't believe she was that. Then I was struck by something that passed between them. It was nothing in itself, only a glance and only from him to her. She was looking at me as she slid the fork between her packed white teeth and I don't know whether she saw it, though she might have sensed it. It was a submissive glance, something I had never associated with Edward, a mute, almost canine submissiveness. It was not the last time I was to see it and it always stood out against the general pattern of her behaviour with him, which was that of a privileged servant who did not protest against his browsing amongst other women. What most surprised me was that it was over questions of writing that he deferred, and I began to feel that in all other areas he operated as it were under licence, albeit a generous one. Nor, so far as I could then see, did she stop him writing what he wanted; it was simply that now and again she would make some surprising and definitive pronouncement on a question of literary provenance or inspiration and Edward would mutely defer. It was not like him—or rather, it was like what he became but not what he had been.

When he showed me out that night we stood talking at the door for a while. For the first time since I had known him I sensed he was making small talk. We stood on the steps and talked Victorian architecture; we watched the wind blow rubbish along the street and talked of contemporary slovenliness; I think we might even have talked about the stars, as the next thing to look at, had not this change in Edward struck me enough to make me bold. I asked again what he thought the writing noise was caused by.

He watched a newspaper being blown along the railings. It made half-hearted and unavailing attempts to save itself as it was harried ever farther down the street. "It's probably my imagination," he said slowly. "When I'm thinking, you know. A projection of some sort like a poltergeist."

"You've heard it before?"

"Don't mention it to anyone, especially not to Eudoxie."

"I suppose it might frighten her."

He glanced at me, then back at the paper.

"Have I seen Eudoxie before?" I asked. "With Tyrrel?"

"Don't talk about that. She'd be very upset."

It was hard to imagine Eudoxie upset but I didn't say anything. There were questions I wanted to ask—how had he come by her, where was she when Tyrrel died, where was she from, had she really embraced someone (Edward?) in that upstairs room—but I could see he didn't want to answer. Yet neither did he seem to want to part and we lingered a few more minutes. I think we talked about Lambeth Council.

The next year or so resembled its predecessor so closely that it is hard to distinguish them. Chantal and I lived as we had and Edward lived as he had, so far as I could tell. Eudoxie seemed to make no difference to the outward form of his life although I called less often. I felt inhibited by her presence, even in the background, as if I were intruding, yet nothing in Edward's demeanour or hers suggested I was. We had them to dinner once, and they us. On neither occasion was anyone else present.

I heard the writing noise only once more during that period. At the time I wondered if I had imagined it but I now believe I did not. I was alone in Edward's room, waiting for him. The book he was writing was just a few sheets on his desk—that was during his first longhand period—and I had to force myself not to look at it. I was always intensely curious about how writers worked, how often they crossed out and so on. The manuscript that Tyrrel had passed on was also there but I saw it as simply a heap of bound papers in someone else's handwriting and took no notice. I sat in the usual chair and, in the usual silence, listened to see if I could hear the scratching again. After a while I thought I could, faintly at first but getting stronger. It was as before: regular, punctuated, rapid, the sound of a prolific and relentless pen. Edward startled me by opening the door and the noise went. I do not say it stopped because there was something about it that made me suspect it was always there, waiting to be heard. Edward glanced sharply at me but we began talking and the moment passed.

I know now that he often heard it. It did not begin with his possession of the manuscript although that was the essential preliminary. I learned all this when he gave me his third account of Tyrrel's death, near the end. In his first two accounts he did not mention Eudoxie but in fact she was there when Tyrrel died. During those moments while Tyrrel and Edward were facing each other beside the desk, each holding the manuscript, Eudoxie appeared at Edward's side. He felt her before he saw her. She stood just behind his left shoulder, very close, and she neither moved nor spoke. It was because of her, Edward thought, that he had had the impression that Tyrrel was looking at him but seeing something else; and it was because of her, he became convinced, that Tyrrel's eyes filled with horror.

He never was sure how much time passed between Tyrrel's backward fall and his own first movement. It may have been much longer than it felt. He came to himself as if from a trance and looked round for Eudoxie but she was not there. The only indication that she had been was that the door was left open. She must have come in for the death.

His immediate thought was that he could not now steal the manuscript and, in the way we all have, he convinced himself that he had never seriously intended to steal it anyway. But he did not let go of it and he looked at the first pages while standing by the body. Like me, he was unable at first to make any sense of it. The neat, spiky writing was legible so long as he focused on individual letters but when he tried to see a word, phrase or sentence whole it became gibberish. Nor was it a normal gibberish, as it were, but a sickening, dizzy-making miasma which at the same time seemed unaccountably and unpleasantly familiar, like a reminder during waking moments of a forgotten dream.

He left Tyrrel and went in search of Eudoxie, taking the manuscript. All the other ground-floor rooms were unlit and he began to wonder if he had imagined her presence. He didn't switch on any lights because the curtains were drawn back and the moonlight came in from the bay, so that the house was more in deep shadow than darkness. Eventually he called out. He had shaken hands with her on arrival but Tyrrel had not named her so he was reduced to calling out "Hallo" and "Excuse me" in English and French.

"Up here," she called, in English.

It was the room in which I had seen her during the storm and in which I thought I saw her the night after. It was a bedroom. She was standing before the big window, facing the bay and the lights of Villefranche, her arms folded as when I watched her. Edward remembered that thin streaks of cloud were drifting across the moon. She did not turn when he entered.

"You have it with you?" she asked.

He knew what she meant. "Yes."

"It is for you. He wanted you to have it."

"Why? How do you know?"

"It was his wish."

"But what is it? I can't make sense of it."

"I will show you. You will have me too."

"What do you mean?" It was surprise that made him ask. When she turned he could see by the whiteness of her teeth that she was smiling.

"I come with it."

Edward spent the night there, and the next day and

the next night, which was why he did not turn up at M. Englert's to meet us. He said later that Eudoxie might have stood in the window the night following with her arms folded, as I thought I saw from the garden, and that she might have turned to embrace him. There were many embraces. But there were other possible explanations.

"You don't always see what Eudoxie does at the time she does it," he said. "Put another way, you may see what but not always when. You saw her on the second night but she may have done it on the first. Perhaps she just wanted you to see her and so you did. Or perhaps she wanted to see you."

"Why should she?"

By the time we had this conversation Edward's blue eyes were as watery as old Tyrrel's. "Because you were associated with me and she needed to make sure."

"Of what?"

"That you weren't important."

Edward and Eudoxie were alone in that house for some thirty-six hours. They were interrupted by the undertakers the next morning and by the need to make statements to the police. They pretended that Edward had neither spent the night there nor been present at the time of Tyrrel's death, matters which Eudoxie handled with her customary efficiency. Otherwise, the two nights and one afternoon passed as minutes, he told me. I believe the presence of Tyrrel's body made the first night particularly fervid. I am not sure that he and Eudoxie had a sexual relationship after that time. Perhaps they did—one can never know—but Edward spoke of it as a time of sexual obsession, if not slavery, and gave the impression that by so indulging they had got sex out of the way for good. Certainly, his later philandering was more in the nature of samplings than adventures, bites from apples not so much in hope of a new taste as to confirm the old. There were many apples but I suspect Eudoxie had inoculated him against any new taste.

The scratching, the writing sound, did not begin until he was back in London. At first he thought it was something to do with his room, expansion in the heating pipes or even mice in the ceiling, but then he noticed that it occurred only when he was writing or thinking about writing. Even then he still sought an everyday explanation but the rhythm and the sound of page after page being filled by an unfaltering pen ruled out everything normal. Whenever he sat down to write he would wait, pen in hand, for the sounds to start, and his own thoughts were strangled at birth. He tried writing with music playing, which he would have found difficult enough anyway, but the scratching made itself heard through, as he put it, his mind's ear. He tried working in the kitchen but it followed him. He was getting desperate by the time Eudoxie arrived.

She was with him much sooner after Tyrrel's death than I had known. She must have been there during our talks. Although the manuscript still baffled him whenever he looked at it—which he did often though never for long because of the sickening properties of the gibberish—and although the scratching continued, her presence made an immediate difference. Now, when he looked at the manuscript or heard the noise, his head filled with words, scenes, characters, voices and echoes in such profusion that he felt he couldn't contain them. All he could do was to siphon them off through his own pen, writing automatically with hardly a shaping thought of his own. That is how he started the fashion for so-called fictive realism which made him so famous and rich. He had only to sit and wait for the sounds or turn the pages of the gibberish for it all to rush into his head like water from a sluice, and then he had simply to open his pen. As he went on the process became ever easier and he became immensely prolific and successful, as we know; but his own thoughts and his own imagination perished.

It was because of what was happening that he wouldn't move to better premises in those early years. He associated it at first not only with Eudoxie but with those Victorian rooms, and feared to lose it. He still thought he could drop it when he wanted and he was intrigued and excited, enjoying his success. He thought he had stumbled upon something new and persuaded himself that when eventually he returned to his own writing he would be enriched. But he remained wary of discussing it. I made a few attempts after that dinner with Eudoxie, only to find him at first offhand and later brusque, as if he had no time for such nonsense.

Chapter 5

CHANTAL AND I moved to Antibes some months after the birth of our first daughter. I got a job in the *lycée* and she was able to work part-time teaching French to foreigners. In the first flush of parental enthusiasm we both felt that London was no place to bring up children. They should live in small towns with easy access to countryside or sea—as should adults, ideally. Also, climate is very important. If it is right it makes everything else better but if it is wrong nothing else will really do and the daily condition of life is struggle.

In fact, the summers in Antibes are too hot for my taste but they suited Chantal. With help from her father, we got an apartment in the same block as her parents. This meant that her sister, Catherine, now a tall and lissom young woman, was available for baby-sitting. So life was pleasant; indeed, being away from

London and that dreadful school was like permanent holiday. Work was no longer onerous and stressful but something one just did, like shaving or making coffee. I could walk to the *lycée* every day along by the harbour.

Some time after the birth of our second daughter, Edward and Eudoxie moved to Villefranche. They reoccupied Tyrrel's house which I assumed was left to Eudoxie though I did read something in the papers about a will that was disputed by one or two of his former wives; but the wife or wives died and whatever fuss there was fizzled out. Eudoxie had it.

I was delighted, of course, though I did not see as much of Edward as I had thought I would. It is a commonplace that children so weaken friendships that many parents cease to be social beings at all. Meetings and conversations become rather desperate occasions, an exchange of notes and a hurried scramble to run up some semblance of the old self. Chantal and I were more fortunate, not only because we had her family on hand but because she was well-organized and efficient, almost Teutonic. She appreciated that time and space have to be created and that neither occurs if you wait for them, so she made sure that there was always some time in the week for doing what she wanted. I was the more willing to help with this because she understood that I needed the same. Perhaps because neither of us felt ourselves to be a natural parent, whatever that is, we saw to it that things worked.

I saw Edward about once a month. I would get the train or drive to Villefranche, though sometimes he would have reason to be in Antibes and we would meet at M. Englert's. Only once or twice did he come to our flat; the presence of children, even signs of their existence such as toys or the push-chair in the hall, discomforted him. As often with people who have an ambition in life, the whole business of families was irrelevant. Nor did Eudoxie ever show any interest in children though she was, I was told, hospitable and charming when Chantal and Catherine occasionally took them over to Villefranche for an afternoon.

It was at first strange for me to sit in the room where I had seen Tyrrel with his head in his hands. The house was larger than appeared from outside and had a balcony, shielded by the extension from the steps that went down the side of the garden. Edward and I would talk on the balcony in the evenings, looking across the bay to the white buildings of Villefranche. He had put on weight and was fuller in the face. I suppose I was, too, but the journey from youth to early middle age is barely perceptible from within. Anyway, it seemed appropriate that he should put on more weight than I did since he was more prosperous. Chantal and I were far from hard-up thanks to her father and we lived in an apartment we could never otherwise have afforded, but we were not in the same league as Edward and Eudoxie. Edward's royalties were huge and it is possible that Eudoxie also benefited from a share of Tyrrel's. Several of Edward's books were filmed and he wrote a couple of the scripts himself. They were highly acclaimed but they lacked the almost chaotic energy and fantasy that informed his novels. Despite exotic photography and apparently arbitrary cutting, they were like watered-down versions of the books. He did no more scripts after those two, saying that a film was necessarily a group production rather than the work of an individual and, in any case, was really made in the cutting-room. Certainly, the scripts lacked the peculiarly strong stamp of individuality we used to think of as his.

Our talks became less literary with the years. I imagine this was in part a natural waning of youthful enthusiasm; like other passions, that for things of the mind rarely survives the avalanche of success or, in my case, the accumulation of domestic responsibilities. It was Conrad, I think, who wrote about how good it was, how free, to be young and to have nothing, and I can almost believe it. But to be old and have nothing benefits no one; the silting up of arteries with money and property is not always the malign process that some people think, and the daily accretion of detail, the one-damn-thing-after-another of it all, is more a part of life than all the great themes.

The other reason our talks became less literary was what was happening to Edward. It was not so much that he was distracted by success or circumstance as that a deadliness invaded the very heart of his genius and spread from there to occupy every part of his life, so that in time there was almost nothing for him to oppose it with. In his very struggles to free himself, it was becoming him. As the years passed, I sensed that our talks became more important. This was not because of what was said, since their content was increasingly insubstantial, but because they took place regularly and because I had known him in his early days, before it all started. I was his only contact with his former life, I alone survived his success; nothing else of his past, of himself—really nothing, by the end—remained to him.

I was touched and grateful that he appeared so to value our talks but I didn't ask myself why. I accepted them as sessions of mutual reassurance and comfort while in the background his reputation as another Tyrrel blossomed. That had a momentum of its own, seemingly no more to do with him than with me, which in a sense was the case. In the curious way of the media, Edward's self-rationed appearances on radio and television were taken as evidence for rather than against his having adopted Tyrrel's reclusive mantle, and he was never introduced without being said to have come out of seclusion especially for that programme.

I remember little of what we used to discuss. Local politics featured, since Chantal's father was involved and it was a neutral and untaxing subject about which we could be indignant and scornful without being challenged to act. World politics was a more regular subject, as it often is among people for whom the personal is either impoverished or for some reason to be avoided. I have noticed that a preoccupation with current affairs sometimes develops among mentally active people who feel that life is slipping away from them or passing them by. I don't think Edward felt this and I know I didn't at that time but we both nevertheless avoided the personal. I'm not sure why; perhaps Edward's reluctance to talk about himself affected me or perhaps we both avoided that of which we sensed there was no ultimate resolution, dissatisfaction being more a matter of temperament than circumstance. Not that Edward ever had any serious political enthusiasms. He had not the nature of an enthusiast, he did not love to hate and his manner was always sceptical, even where his words were not. More even than before, he gave his opinions in inverted commas, which made it sound as if he did not trust the words he used.

I have clearer memories of the circumstances of our talks than of the subjects. Barbecues on the balcony with the moon on the water, lunches in the garden beneath the shade of the olive trees, sometimes a wood fire in Edward's study and always wine, plenty of wine, and afterwards whisky. He drank a lot but my own increase prevented me from noticing quite how much he was taking. He had continued to smoke cigars ever since that morning we had met at M. Englert's after Tyrrel's death. They might even have been Tyrrel's cigars to start with; whether they were or not, he smoked them with the same careless compulsion, discarding them before the end.

One of the occasions that stands out was an evening on the balcony. The sun had set, leaving a clear but fading light. Eudoxie was gardening—she was a keen gardener and often used to work in the cool of the evening—and Edward had gone inside to get another bottle of whisky. I could hear him moving about downstairs as I sat smoking one of his cigars and watching Eudoxie. She was wearing jeans and a white T-shirt which showed up in the fading light. Her hair was loose and hung over her face as she bent to do something to a plant. She had to keep pushing it back with one hand, which reminded me of the first time I saw her with Tyrrel and brought me to reflect upon how lucky she was to be one of those women who seem ageless. Chantal, of course, had had motherhood to contend with but even without that would have been as obviously in early middle age as I was. Even Catherine, whom I still tended to think of as never being more than twelve, was now more woman than girl. But Eudoxie remained as vital and as elusive as ever.

She straightened and turned to face the house, raising one hand as if to shade her eyes. There was really no need and I think she had probably reached to pat her hair and had simply not lowered her hand. In her other she held a trowel. She was looking at the big window of Edward's study. I could no longer hear him moving but I could hear the sounds of a typewriter. It was neither loud nor particularly rapid but it was regular, as if the typist used only two fingers but was quite practised. Edward had mentioned that he typed now rather than wrote. I thought it odd that he should leave me and work, but who was I to question the ways of great writers? My once passionate belief that art transcended social obligation had settled into a habit of thought every bit as unreflecting as any convention. The sounds could not have lasted very long because I remember I had not finished my cigar when they stopped and Edward reappeared. Eudoxie was bending over the plants again.

I told Edward he shouldn't worry about me but should carry on with his work if he wanted; I was happy with the whisky and the view.

He looked puzzled. "I could hear you typing," I added.

He stood with the bottle in his hand. "Just now?"

"When you were downstairs. Eudoxie could, too. At least, she was staring at you in the study."

He glanced at her, not exactly fearfully but as a sailor might glance at clouds. "It wasn't me," he said quietly.

"But you do type your stuff now, don't you?"

"I've been trying it." He put the bottle on the table and sat heavily in the wicker chair. For a while he sat and stared as if he were alone. His features had sagged of late and his belly bulged over the top of his trousers but he was still a handsome man. When he brooded, as now, it was easy to imagine him as a Henry VIII, unpredictable, capable equally of impulsive generosity or quiet vindictiveness, according to the heaviness within.

"It has taken the place of the writing noise," he said eventually. "It wasn't me typing but I was thinking about it. It started when I changed to the typewriter. You are the only person apart from Eudoxie who knows about this." His blue eyes rested vacantly upon mine.

"Does it help to type? Do you feel you write better?"

"I cannot write at all. Whatever I do comes out nonsense. It doesn't like me leaving the pen."

"Perhaps you should try a word processor."

He shook his head, opened the bottle and poured.

I regretted the flippancy of my remark because I very much wanted to know more but I had been puzzled by his words and a little frightened by his manner. It was like being with someone who had identified in himself the symptoms of fatal illness and you wish to jolly him out of it, while suspecting he might be right. I did not then know how completely the writing had taken possession of him and when he spoke of "it" not wanting him to forsake the pen I feared he was displaying symptoms of a nervous condition. It was also about that time that I began to suspect that he was profoundly lacking in self-awareness. At first I thought this odd in a writer but now I am not so sure; if you study their books as I do you will often see what they do not. The effect of Edward's unselfconsciousness, if I can call it that, was to create the illusion of quiet decisiveness, determination, sureness of purpose. It also suggested an incipient brutality which I think some people found attractive. Yet at the same time it somehow made one feel *for* him as if he were a child in this world. We

83

might all have felt more for him if we had had any idea of the emptiness, destruction and terror concealed beneath his heavy immobility, his measured tones, and his apparently attentive blue eyes.

He did actually get a word processor though I know he never wrote a book on it. What was taken to be his reluctance to embrace new technology became a part of the mythology and it was sometimes contrasted with the way in which he was always abreast or ahead of literary fashion. No one had any idea then that the word processor represented a desperate attempt to escape his fate; it was regarded as his one concession to modernity. His surroundings, notwithstanding the luxury of the view, remained spartan. He and Eudoxie occupied that house as if they had never properly unpacked and I think that was how he came to view his place in the world. The walls were as bare as his Kennington flat, there was little furniture, no television and no sound system. Presumably there must have been a number of Tyrrel's effects but I never saw any. I gathered that Eudoxie looked after everything connected with the property. How she viewed her place in the world, none can know.

I discovered the word processor by accident. Whether my remark had influenced Edward, I have no idea; he had said nothing about getting one. It was a Saturday and Chantal and I had taken the children for lunch with cousins of hers in Villefranche. Parents with young children are not often welcome—at least, there is usually more genuine pleasure at their departure than their arrival—but these cousins had enough children for two more to make little difference. From their house we could make out Edward's across the bay as two white rectangles, one horizontal and one vertical, with red roofs and windows that caught the sun. The green Cap was dotted with many larger white and red shapes but there was none more famous. Edward had recently removed the name from outside the house because of the number of thesis-hunters who found their way up the steps or along the lane. On that Saturday afternoon we thought we could call on him. I was wary of doing so unannounced but Chantal thought it all right provided we left the children with her cousins.

We walked round the bay and up the lane as when we had followed Tyrrel and Eudoxie all those years before, so we arrived at the front of the house without having seen into the garden. The door was answered by Eudoxie, wearing only a red towel. Her skin was darker than I had thought and for a moment we all three stared at each other. She was surprised and perhaps momentarily irritated; something crossed her face. However, it left no trace behind and she was immediately polite and welcoming. She paid more attention to Chantal than to me but that was not uncommon. She led us through the house and up to the balcony, calling out our arrival as we went. We reached the balcony in time to see Catherine covering her nakedness in a red towel like Eudoxie's. She had obviously been lying on it near to Edward who sat in a wicker chair reading a paper. His feet were bare and he wore khaki drill trousers, a white shirt unbuttoned to the waist and a khaki hat which shielded his eyes. The two women must have lain naked at his feet, sun-bathing.

I think Chantal and I were too surprised to be embarrassed. We stared for a moment and then I said that we hadn't known Catherine would be there, and yielded to my English instinct for apology. I knew that both my talent for stating the obvious and my impulse to apologize irritated Chantal but I couldn't help it at that moment; I thought that that accounted for her taciturnity during the tea that ensued. Catherine said nothing and went inside to dress but Eudoxie remained, the towel wrapped precariously around her. She was spirited and friendly and, as always when she laughed, I could not help noticing how her small white teeth filled her mouth. They were so even and so many that it was as if they had been manufactured and assembled rather than grown. They were not unattractive, rather the reverse; I always wanted to touch them. Anyway, Chantal thawed under Eudoxie's attention and when Eudoxie took her by the hand and said she wanted to show her the wallflowers in the garden she laughed and got to her feet with something like youthful alacrity.

Edward had not put down his paper. He had smiled greetings and had unconcernedly let the chatter happen around him, like so much froth and foam around a rock. When we were alone he said: "Your girls with the cousins?"

I nodded and he resumed reading. It was a companionable silence after all the fuss. There seemed to be nothing to say.

"Drop of whisky?" he asked after a while.

I offered to fetch it from downstairs. As I passed his and Eudoxie's bedroom I caught sight of Catherine dressing. She was wearing white knickers and bra and was pulling on a green skirt. Our eyes met before she looked down to fasten the skirt at her waist. Her glance was as unembarrassed as it was uninterested and it was only then that she at last became, for me, no longer Chantal's little sister but a part of the great half-known world of womanhood. Of course, it was years since she had been anything else so far as Chantal was concerned but I did not appreciate that at the time.

I found the whisky and was about to go back upstairs with it when I was attracted into Edward's darkened study by a green glow. I am not a very perceptive person and perhaps for that reason I feel I have to take an interest in everything. I am, to use the old word, nosy, and cannot pass an open door without looking in. I had not expected to see Catherine in Edward's bedroom but could not resist a glance to see what *was* there. Nor could I resist his study. The curtains were still drawn and the glow came from a computer screen. This was the first I knew of Edward's transition. It was an Amstrad, not a very sophisticated one even by the standards of the day but more than adequate for all that a novelist was likely to need. On the desk beside it was Tyrrel's manuscript, which was still unknown to me. My attention was anyway drawn to the screen. Reproduced there was the malignant gibberish which I later knew to be that of the manuscript, but at the time I thought that either there was something wrong with the software or that Edward did not know what he was doing.

I had been there only a moment when Eudoxie appeared. She stood in the doorway with an expression of intense concentration, staring at the screen. Then she looked at me.

"What are you doing?" she asked.

"I haven't touched anything. I saw the light and wondered what it was."

She came over and stood close enough for her bare shoulder to touch my arm. She took no interest in me but simply stared at the screen. I felt that if her towel had fallen about her feet she would not have moved.

"It doesn't seem to make any sense," I said.

She switched it off. "The others are upstairs."

After we had left, Chantal didn't say anything about Catherine. I knew that Catherine knew Edward and Eudoxie, of course, because she sometimes visited with Chantal, but I had no idea she saw them alone. Eventually I mentioned it.

"She's always thrown herself at him," said Chantal.

"Are they having an affair?"

"I've no idea."

Her tone was offhand, as if the subject were familiar to us both.

We—or rather, Chantal—saw more of Eudoxie after that. They became friends. Eudoxie would come over to Antibes and they would go shopping, or they would lunch, and some afternoons Chantal would go over to Cap Ferrat. Now and again Eudoxie would just drop in for coffee, bringing something for the children, whom she charmed. I don't know whether Catherine continued to visit Cap Ferrat; she ceased to feature in anyone's conversation. Later I discovered that she was having an affair with one of my married colleagues from the *lycée*. When I told Chantal she nodded, as if we were both familiar with that, too.

"Yes, it's time she put a stop to that. It's been going

on since she was seventeen. He's far too old and he'll never leave his wife. I've told her, Eudoxie's told her, but she doesn't listen. She'll have to find out the hard way."

"She's in love with him, then?"

"She thinks she is."

I do not pretend to understand these matters but I was pleased that Chantal was seeing more of Eudoxie because it appeared to cheer her. She had become tense and taciturn, particularly with me, and for no reason that she would vouchsafe. She would make such remarks as, "The trouble with you is you don't want anything," but when I tried to find out what it was I was supposed to want she would become annoyed. Living with someone who appears to bear a permanent grudge is hard, especially when your ignorance of the cause is held against you, and failure to understand the other party is a charge against which there is no possibility of defence. Indeed, it is hard not to give way to resentment when you feel that you, too, may be misunderstood, or that your wife understands herself no better than she thinks you do. Physical relations between us virtually ceased.

Of course, I had no idea what misery she was living in and, suspecting that ours was not an uncommon marital condition, I put it down to the approach of early menopause; my suspicions were increased rather than lessened by her enraged denials. As for myself, it is not always easy to describe one's feelings for someone one lives with day in and day out for years. When two people are so interpenetrated it is difficult to know where one ends and the other begins. Though worried by her unhappiness, I was not in myself unhappy; I jogged along, which was part of what she seemed to have against me.

But when she started seeing more of Eudoxie she became brighter and recovered a good deal of her humour. I assumed that Eudoxie supplied feminine companionship in place of Catherine, and I was half right. The four of us—Edward, Eudoxie, Chantal and myself—became more of a foursome than we had been and met more often. It seemed a good arrangement.

The incident with the word processor remained present to my mind partly because of Edward's next book, which was publicized as being the first he had written—actually, "composed" was the word used—electronically. This was the book that established him as a literary writer of truly international status, a highbrow bestseller. No one since Thomas Mann, I would guess, not even Tyrrel, had so combined sales with intellectual repute. Yet to me that book represented a falling-off. It rambled and, for all its ingenuity, left an impression of inconsequentiality. At first I put it down to the word processor, delighted to confirm—as I thought—a prejudice. It is my belief that people who compose on word processors are beguiled by the medium and write longer, looser, less concentrated works. Then I was puzzled, though not shaken in my belief, to discover that Edward had not used the word processor after all. I had made some remark about it, preparatory to tactful criticism, and he said, "Oh, that. No, I couldn't get on with it. I sent it back."

I was surprised that he had permitted the publicity about his using one, supposedly so long after most writers, but he just shrugged. It was only later when he told me about the gibberish that I learned that this, like his typing, had been another failed attempt to regain his own voice. The writing, the manuscript, the scratching, would not let him go. Everything he tried on the machine came out as gibberish. He would begin a normal sentence, pressing what he thought were the right keys, and the green screen would show nonsense. He knew it was not the machine, which had been demonstrated to work, but something within him. He tried typing the gibberish exactly as he read it in the manuscript, to see if it would come out sense as it did when he used his pen, but it would not translate. That was the experiment I saw. It—whatever it was—was as jealous of other forms of transcription as of his having ideas of his own. He was blocked, driven back to the scratching and his own pen. Thus the book that was hailed as such a success was, for Edward, utter defeat.

The most important defect of that book, though, was its lack of honesty. Honesty is what gives a book its centre of gravity and if it lacks it, though it has all the other virtues, it will be forever pretending to be something it never quite is. That, at least, is my opinion and it was because of that book that I began re-reading its predecessors with a different eye. What I saw reminded me of what he had said about Tyrrel's work being a dance around emptiness. That is now, of course, the conventional view of Edward's work. I record this not to claim prescience but because I want to show how a potentially great writer was destroyed and because I am sure it did not begin with Tyrrel or end with Edward.

He was aware of the book's faults. One evening we dined alone at Englert's and lingered until most of the customers had gone. The shutters were closed and M. Englert sat with some friends at the big table, talking football. I felt relaxed enough to be nearly frank. I told Edward that his book struck me as more of a contrivance than the others—skilful, entertaining, with dazzling language and wit but in the end less meaning.

"Sound and fury signify not nothing but nothingness," he said. "That is the point."

"You did it deliberately?"

"It was deliberate." He spoke carefully. "There is nothing accidental in my books."

"Of course not."

"No, not of course. With most writers there is much that is accidental. They reveal themselves in every other sentence. They can't help it and they don't always know what they're revealing but they have to do it because for them it's part of the process. Yet what do you see of me in my writing?"

It was true that there was nothing of Edward as I knew him, but what did I know of him? Not much when I thought about it, and I realized that I regarded his novels as characteristic of him only because they resembled each other; there was no point at which they seemed to attach to him. But still I did not fully understand what he was saying. I thought he meant to be the kind of artist Joyce wrote about, Godlike, remote, refined almost out of existence, paring his fingernails.

He shook his head. "I mean that my writing is nothing to do with me."

"You regard it all as an experiment, then?"

"That is how it started."

I learned no more that night. Now I know what a driven man he was, unable to write a word of his own even in a letter, possessed, stifled, terrified, I can only admire the way he continued to fight it when others,

Tyrrel among them, must have acquiesced. His apparent self-possession was really the fragile stasis of an ancient vase and if he had let himself be moved, or show feeling, he would have broken into a thousand pieces. He came as close as he dared to telling me on that occasion but until the very end his fear of Eudoxie held him back. He was her prisoner; she surrounded him with everything he wanted and in exchange she and that manuscript took possession of his soul. As time went by he wanted less and less of other things, desiring only the one thing he could not have. He tried to fight them but you need spirit to fight and it was his spirit they claimed. How he kept on I do not know; but I do know that during all those years when I was seeing my friend what I took for the calm acceptance of worldly success and the clear-sighted indifference of genius was in fact the stillness of near-catatonic frenzy, the quiet of near-total despair.

The Antibes years, as I think of them, came to an end when Edward and Eudoxie announced they were going to travel. We did not know how long a break this was to be and I don't think they did either. We imagined they would go round the world for a year or so. Chantal and I stayed, of course, but I never think of our remaining years there as Antibes years, more a kind of footnote. The great events had happened already.

The night before Edward and Eudoxie were to leave

there was a buzz on our entryphone. I was surprised to hear Edward's distorted voice since it was unprecedented for him to drop by. I went out into the corridor to meet the lift but he ran up the stairs. He was flabby and untidy, his face was red and his hair wet with exertion. He wore a light suit that had had something spilt on the trousers and his tie was askew. He was breathing heavily.

"I can't stop, I'm in a hurry," he said. "I wondered if you'd look after this for me until I get back." He handed me a manuscript in a supermarket carrier bag. "Didn't want to leave it in the house. Too heavy to cart around. Got enough as it is."

I had never seen him hurried or flustered. Chantal stood just behind me, saying nothing. He left no time for questions.

"Thanks," he said. "Be in touch." He ran back down the stairs.

I know now that the manuscript was the one he had from Tyrrel but I didn't look at it that night, hindered by some rare scruple—which no doubt I should have overcome the next day—and anyway distracted by Chantal.

"She's driven him away," she said.
"Who?"
"Eudoxie."
"But she's going with him."

"I don't care. She's driving him away." She went into our bedroom and shut the door.

The next morning the buzzer went again but this time it was Eudoxie. We had just finished breakfast and I was about to leave for school. She wanted to come up, she said. Edward had left a manuscript last night which he had now decided he wanted; also, she wanted to say goodbye.

"Tell her you'll take it down with you," said Chantal.

"Don't you want to say goodbye?"

"You say it for me." She got up and went into the kitchen.

The girls were also ready for school and so they came down with me. Eudoxie was smiling and calm, quite unlike Edward. She made a fuss of the girls, promising them all sorts of things from abroad and complimenting them on their appearance. Her own was striking: she wore a white, tightly waisted suit, her hair was pinned back, her dark eyes just sufficiently emphasized, her lipstick bright and from her ears swayed pendulous gold medallions. What in most women would seem too cosmetic in her came into its own. She was laughing and charming and the girls were entranced. She was even mildly flirtatious with me.

"My love as always to Chantal," she said, kissing me lightly on the lips.

I held her hand for a moment too long. She smiled

97

and turned to the girls. She could have passed for
twenty.

EDWARD AND EUDOXIE were itinerant from then on.
They kept the house at Cap Ferrat and occasionally re-
visited but never for long. When I saw him there was
never much said. Not that there needed to be. Our
friendship was an acknowledgement that we went back
a long way, that there was more behind than to come.
I don't think either of us had the linear view of relation-
ships which demands progression towards—well,
what? That is always the problem.

He put on more weight and became a heavy, bloated
figure although his basic good looks could still be
traced beneath the distended flesh. His skin became
red and shiny, his hair silvery and thin but his eyes kept
their colour—blue and white islands in a red and wrinkled sea. He stared unblinkingly at whomever spoke to
him, still giving the impression that he was concentrating the full force of his attention. His movements became stiff and slow and he would often simply sit and
stare. He developed a sort of woodenness and I kept
expecting to see him with a stick, which I never did
despite his adopting a blue blazer and cavalry twills.
Eudoxie of course was unchanged and if she sometimes
wore the clothes of an older woman it was, one felt, in

deference to Edward's ageing rather than from any need to acknowledge her own.

And still the books came, if anything at a faster rate than before. Whether from Bali or Belgrade, Auckland, Rome or Ruidoso, they tumbled out, along with streams of interviews, articles, prizes and occasional news stories. He became a more public figure though his appearances were punctuated by wanderings in remote places. Sometimes his whereabouts would be unknown for months at a time, but Eudoxie never left him and the travelling, given his condition, could not have been arduous. I suppose he could afford to make it comfortable.

The books of his last years were his most popular and even now, when his work is so out of fashion, some are still read. Products of his restless journeyings, they have at their best an elegiac quality, a blending of fact and fiction that soothes because it discourages judgement and makes criticism seem out of place. It never is, of course, and they do not really work because they are not the real thing; at the base of all that fantasy is heartlessness. It is curious that we who deify the concept of the individual should devalue people, encouraging conformity, starving imagination. We no longer imagine in order to see more deeply, only to block off, to escape from having to see at all, and the essential evil of all Edward's fantasies is that under the pretence of illuminating, they in fact diminish. Not that they were really his, of course.

I cannot read them now. At the time I read most of them but the late ones I ignored. By then I would have found it pretty hard to read anything by Edward, even if it had been truly good. Being cuckolded is doubtless a more common experience than is realized and, like other upsets in life, its effects are not always what might be thought. When Chantal told me I didn't feel anger or even great surprise. I waited for both as if, until I had felt them, I hadn't properly reacted. What I did feel was an inner blankness from which no echo came; later a prolonged and growing disappointment which lasted for years and turned many things bitter. Insofar as the past is your life and your memory is what you are, the discovery that large chunks of both are not and never were what you thought demands a pretty fundamental revision if you are to go on with any sense of self intact. I had always been afraid that I was incapable of anger—which lack is not a virtue, though control of anger would be—and this confirmed it. I was also afraid that even in youth I had been a bit of an old fuddy-duddy who bored people, and this did nothing to reassure me.

Mind you, the way it came out was hardly dramatic and natures more volatile than my own might still have suffered only a delayed reaction. It was many years after the episode—I still have difficulty with the word "affair"—and Chantal mentioned it in a moment of such deep unhappiness and self-concern that any immediate response I might have made was neutered; she probably wouldn't have noticed. It happened on the night after the wedding of our younger daughter. Our elder daughter was married already and the younger had been living away from home for some time, but she had always been Chantal's favourite. I imagine the marriage confirmed what Chantal must have known but had not wanted to face—that her children needed her no longer, that the chicks had flown the nest. It must be hard for many women to find that after years of being demanded of and depended upon they are simply left, thenceforth to be remembered, if they are lucky, with polite consideration and occasional affection. At any rate, when we returned to our flat after a long and tiring reception it was uncomfortable to be alone and silent. Chantal wept. I tried to comfort her but her weeping became increasingly uncontrolled until eventually she said, between sobs:

"I haven't felt like this since Edward left me."

The whole story did not come out then, but I shall spare you the detail and myself the memory. She had always been what she called "interested" in Edward although the business did not begin until after the incident with Catherine. She had been seduced—I use the word deliberately—into it by Eudoxie. So too, I suspect, had Catherine and most of Edward's women. Eudoxie pimped for him, which was another way of maintaining control; no doubt she enjoyed herself at the same time. But what began as flattery, excitement and dalliance became for poor Chantal a passion. I call her "poor" because that is how I used to make myself think of her, as a way of getting over it. She was swept out to sea by an undertow she had never known before, helpless, guilty, wanting to stop, wanting to go on, a prisoner of Eudoxie's keen attentiveness and Edward's supine, tantalizing indifference. It was clear to me that she never mattered to him, that she was just another apple from which he took a bite, but she could never believe it. She convinced herself that he and Eudoxie went abroad because he could not bring himself to finish with her while she lived nearby. I did not disillusion her but I know that he never gave her a thought, that she played no part whatever in his own unhappy self-concern. Curiously, it helped me to know that because although I had not the emotional generosity to feel any great pity for her I was able to make a show of it; and she was pitiable. But I think she sensed the truth despite herself, and that broke her utterly.

Chapter 6

❧ I COULD HAVE REMAINED in France but I wanted a complete break from old associations. Chantal stayed in Antibes and the two girls lived with their husbands nearby. That suited them all. I went to London and did a series of supply-teaching or temporary jobs. For a while I didn't even read newspapers in case I saw something about Edward.

It was a pretty wretched time but I wanted to be alone and uncommitted, rootless, with no background and no past, and I came close to realizing it. People are surprisingly incurious once it is clear that you do not wish to be forthcoming; I suppose they find it not worth the effort and, anyway, they have their own lives to live. London is a good city if you want to be alone.

After about eighteen months of this I began to come out of it and started applying for permanent posts. The rapid accumulation of rejections was a dispiriting sign of how much I had aged. So many years outside the

English educational system meant that it was useless to seek jobs of the seniority I should have achieved and I discovered that I had suffered irreparably in pension terms. Eventually, I was invited to interview for a post in Knaresborough, Yorkshire. This cheered me because I didn't usually get as far as an interview.

I liked Knaresborough from the moment I got off the train. It is still attractive despite recent expansion, with some solid old buildings, a market square, a river and a ruined castle. I stayed overnight in a small hotel near the square and late the following afternoon, after my interview, I went for a walk around the town. I felt I had done quite well and now at last I dared hope that I could stop being the permanently temporary, grey visitor of staffrooms, the one for whom another cup had always to be found.

So far from dampening my spirits, the raw wet Yorkshire afternoon gave me something to relish. If you forsake somewhere with the colour and vividness of Antibes you may as well go for its opposite, and this no-nonsense, not unfriendly northern town was quite close to that. I found even the damp dwindling light satisfying. There are many lights and half-lights in such a climate and I had already begun to feel that I was inhabiting a world of ghosts. It suited me.

What is left of the castle occupies the highest point of the town, with the river and railway far below. When

I went there the mist was breeding a fine rain and dusk was closing in. There was only one other person, an old man who walked slowly round the perimeter. Few who live in a place bother with its ruins on a wet afternoon and those that do may be harmless but are often better avoided. If we allow the lonely and the lost to detain us for long we sink with them, before our proper time. That, at least, was how I felt then.

We had actually passed before we recognized each other. It took a few steps for each to place the faded lines of the other drifting wreck. Edward was corpulent, had heavy unshaven jowls and dragged one foot because his shoe had no lace. He wore an old tweed hat and a dirty duffel coat. His cheeks were very red and his blue eyes bloodshot. I had on my best suit for the interview and must have looked respectable but I was a greyer, older man than he might have thought, with bags under my eyes and teeth not my own.

We stood and stared with no greeting. There was nothing to be said. It was not embarrassing but it was sad in a quite impersonal way, as if it were life itself that was fading.

"Do you live here?" he asked at last. They were the same precise tones but hoarse now. I explained what I was doing. "I live here," he said. "Come and have a drink."

I had forgotten that he came from Yorkshire. "Near

Harrogate" was all that he had ever said and I hadn't known that that meant Knaresborough. We went down through the town towards the river. He walked slowly, which gratified me. In the lights of the shops he looked even more like a tramp; no one would have believed he was a multi-millionaire. I had to keep insisting to myself that what had happened between him and Chantal really had happened, because when I looked at him or when he was talking—which, uncharacteristically, he did all the way, proffering a detailed, coherent, unrequested history of the town—the whole business seemed an irrelevance, nothing to do with either of us.

He led us down a steep hill to where the River Nidd cuts through a wooded gorge on the edge of the town. We did not cross the old bridge but turned left into the narrow road that runs by the river. It was by then dark and the road was unlit. We passed a few cottages and one or two larger houses. That lane is now a fashionable and expensive part of town and the houses have carports or garages but then it was dark, uneven and solitary, and quite soon the only sounds were of the river. After the houses the lane ran through tall trees and was bounded on the right by a stone wall. To the left the rockface rose steeply. Edward continued his local history in a voice that seemed indecently loud in such solitude. It was raining steadily by then and during his pauses I could hear the pitter-patter upon thousands of leaves.

He turned abruptly to the right, leaving me to follow more by voice than sight through a gate to a small field that bordered the river where it curved away. The grass was long and wet and I stumbled over the root of a tree. At the river's edge we reached an old boathouse, a substantial decaying structure which had become Edward's home. I saw it subsequently in daylight. It was an elaborate semi-ruin, a wooden extravagance dating from the turn of the century, resting on brick pillars. It had three large rooms apart from the place for the boats. It was destroyed in the floods not long after.

We went up wooden steps into a long room that stretched the width of the building. In the middle of the floor was an old black kitchen range with a metal flue that ran up through the roof. There was a table, a couple of chairs, a few books and papers, and a considerable quantity of lumber. Edward lit a paraffin lamp which smoked and hissed, then fetched whisky and two mugs from another room. He took off his hat and we sat either side of the table while he poured. We kept our coats on. It was then that he told me all that I have related.

There was more. My description of him as a driven man does him less than justice. For decades what he called "it," the manuscript, and "she," Eudoxie, had enlarged their inexorable invasion. I had been unknowing witness to a few of his failed escapes but the years were full of them. All were unavailing and he had known they would be but he still kept trying; there was something of himself as yet unconquered. Towards the end of his time in Antibes he had become increasingly desperate. Not only was it impossible for him to write anything apart from what was dictated, but he found even his non-writing thoughts invaded. He became unable to control his fantasies, particularly with regard to women. They occupied his mind with hallucinatory force, in public places, when he was talking, when he was listening, so that the real everyday world was being blotted out. The only way he could stop was to fill his mind with drink, though that became less effective the more he was used to it. Next he found that the sexual fantasies that plagued him would be enacted. He had only to think of something for Eudoxie to see to it. Hence his bites out of apples were not the casual indulgences I had assumed but something to which he was driven, time and again, by his possessed imagination. This is not in any way to be envied: he could neither will nor prevent it and, as always when the unreal is made real, it turned to ashes in his mouth. He knew that it would, of course, and so was deprived even of the pleasure of anticipation.

He told me this without the slightest embarrassment. I suppose he was beyond all embarrassment. When I mentioned Chantal he stared, his face bloated and heavy, his watery eyes vague. The rain drummed on the roof.

"Oh yes, Chantal," he said. "How is Chantal?"

"She's all right now. She wasn't for a long time. She had to have psychiatric help. But she's in the same flat and she's got our daughters and family and friends nearby. Unlike me. It's me who has changed."

He went on talking. I think he forgot all about poor Chantal and simply ignored what I said about myself. That was the nearest I ever came to anger but even then I couldn't quite make it. My impulse was punctured by the thought that I had been more concerned with trying to draw attention to myself than with bringing home to him what he had done to Chantal; also by his pathetic, obviously fearful state. He spoke of himself as if from the outside, as of one who only ever acted under compulsion, and he seemed hardly aware of other people. You can see that tendency paralleled in his books, in the steady erosion of individual significance. By the end he could write only about himself and as that entity became possessed and consumed, so he became ever more fantastical. The reality of evil is that it is the opposite of real.

He was driven, too, on that lifelong wave of success. He enjoyed it at first and though he knew it was fraudulent he still felt it was something to do with him. But as the wave went higher and faster he felt both irrelevant and threatened. There was no way off except to confess, which he could not bring himself to do. When he tried to stop the writing happening to him he was filled with such demented fantasy and nonsense, which Eudoxie's presence always threatened to translate into reality, that he felt madness was upon him; and that he feared above all. His enormous popularity and his apparent literary significance were for him the most grotesque parody.

His leaving the manuscript with me that night in Antibes was one of his many attempts to separate it from Eudoxie. He was convinced that it would have nothing like such a hold over him without her presence, but she found him out. Their world trip was one long attempt to escape; he hoped he would give her the slip, that she would light upon someone else and leave him, that in the wanderings he described in his last books he would meet his death.

While still speaking he got up and shuffled into the other room to get more whisky. I was not drunk but I felt I didn't want any more. I was hungry, the boathouse was cold, the floorboards creaked and the rain drummed heavily on the roof. The old kitchen range looked dead beyond recall. My feet were still wet from the grass. When Edward returned with another bottle he brought with him the manuscript and a bright red alarm clock that ticked busily. He put them carefully on the table.

"I am expecting a visitor."

"Do you want me to go?"

"Not yet."

He saw me eyeing the manuscript and smiled. His smile seemed unreal after all this time, a relic of the old Edward. "Don't worry, it's not for you. My only hope is to give it away to another writer. It will not leave me otherwise. It has to have someone it can latch on to, you see. I have found one as I was found, as Tyrrel was found before me. But this one will have a chance because I've separated it from her. The new owner might be able to master it rather than the other way round. That's why she must never know where it has gone."

"How did you get away from her?"

"I jumped off a train."

He was still smiling but his expression was sinister. I experienced one of those momentary disorientations, those mental seismic shifts that make you feel there has been some fundamental change yet leave everything looking the same. It may, of course, have been the whisky or an early sign of the heart condition I now have but I felt again that I was in a dream from which

I was powerless to awake. Remotely, it struck me that perhaps this was how most of Edward's life had seemed to him. I saw his bloodshot face across the table and was suddenly unsure whether this was his great attempt to awaken or whether he was seeking to freeze me into his dream perpetually. As if in slow motion or moving under water, he opened the manuscript and held it before me, turning from page to page. Again I saw that neat, spiky malignancy, the gibberish that was so instantly, sickeningly, nonsensically familiar. I heard the scratching now, not only louder than before but as if from a multitude of pens, generations of nibs, a calligraphic cacophony.

I made myself look away. "Burn it," I said, pointing at the stove. "Put it in there."

He closed it carefully. "I will not be the one to do that." He still grinned but it was as if his lips were drawn back involuntarily. "I must pass it on before she finds me and then I must hide, or she will tear me to pieces."

"How? She can't. Don't let her near you." I was convinced of the real world again. We were in a boathouse, it was raining, the paraffin lamp hissed and smelt. "Chuck it in the river and come with me."

"I can't."

"Let me. I'll do it."

He clutched it into his duffel coat and sat, hunched and rocking as if with a baby. He would not meet my eye or look at my outstretched hand.

Edward's visitor was expected at nine. I left at twenty-to. My last sight of Edward was of his standing at the top of the boathouse steps, the manuscript tightly in both arms, the flickering paraffin light behind him. I was to call again before getting my train in the morning.

I slipped a couple of times in the long grass and it was so dark that I had to grope along the rough stone wall for the gate. Once in the lane I walked as fast as I dared towards the town, several times stepping into deep puddles. The only sound was the rain, steady and drenching. I had not quite reached the bend after which you can see the lights of the bridge and its pub, the Mother Shipton, when a figure passed me in the dark. At first I was aware of it only as a patch of denser dark against the rocks and trees but then I sensed the movement and we may—though this could have been my imagination—have brushed shoulders. We had passed each other before I was really sure it had happened. I turned but saw nothing. All I can say is that it was short and moved quickly. It could have been a woman.

I got that job and since then have lived a silent, sedentary, solitary, private life in Knaresborough; not at all a discontented one. Occasionally I visit Chantal in Antibes. She lives, as people often can, as if much of her life had never happened. I cannot do that, can never let it go, must forever be raking it over.

The inquest verdict on Edward was that he had fallen in the river while drunk; the condition of the corpse was attributed to the battering it received during its time in the rock-strewn Nidd, which was in spate. The manuscript was never found. I know that because I helped the police go through his things.

As is well known, Edward's reputation collapsed from the day of his death. Like Tyrrel's, once seen to be a bubble, it burst. Despite what he did to me and Chantal, a great sadness informs my memory of him and I have written this in order that people be not too harsh. He was one of the lost, and I hope is so no longer.

For the rest, I can only say what I saw, heard and was told. I offer no explanations but I have no doubt that somewhere Eudoxie thrives. Three times since my retirement I have been convinced I saw her in the street and have followed, only to be presented with a different face at the end.

And so now, with time on my hands, I spend most of my days in the public library where I am an assiduous reader of contemporary literature. I seek out those rendered invisible by their own dazzle, the stars that burn brightest when dying within; and I pay particular attention to their spouses and lovers. I know the signs, I know what I am looking for.

BUDDENBROOKS
THE DECLINE OF A FAMILY
by Thomas Mann
Translated by John E. Woods

This masterpiece is an utterly absorbing chronicle of four generations of a German mercantile family. As Thomas Mann charts the Buddenbrooks' decline, he creates a world of exuberant vitality and almost Rabelaisian earthiness.

"Wonderfully fresh and elegant . . . bound to become the definitive English version." —*Los Angeles Times*

Fiction/Literature/0-679-75260-9

LOLITA
by Vladimir Nabokov

The famous and controversial novel that tells the story of the aging Humbert Humbert's obsessive, devouring, and doomed passion for the nymphet Dolores Haze.

"The only convincing love story of our century." —*Vanity Fair*

Fiction/Literature/0-679-72316-1

THE ENGLISH PATIENT
by Michael Ondaatje

During the final moments of World War II, four damaged people come together in a deserted Italian villa. As their stories unfold, a complex tapestry of image and emotion, recollection and observation is woven.

"It seduces and beguiles us with its many-layered mysteries, its brilliantly taut and lyrical prose, its tender regard for its characters." —*Newsday*

Winner of the Booker Prize
Fiction/Literature/0-679-74520-3

OPERATION SHYLOCK
by Philip Roth

In this tour de force of fact and fiction, Philip Roth meets a man who may or may not be Philip Roth. Because *someone* with that name has been touring the State of Israel, promoting a bizarre exodus in reverse, and it is up to Roth to stop him—even if that means impersonating his impersonator.

"A diabolically clever, engaging work . . .the result is a kind of dizzying exhilaration." —*Boston Globe*

Fiction/Literature/0-679-75029-0

VINTAGE   INTERNATIONAL